A COVENTRY COURTSHIP

PHYLLIS TAYLOR PIANKA

Harlequin Books

TORONTO • NEW YORK • LONDON
AMSTERDAM • PARIS • SYDNEY • HAMBURG
STOCKHOLM • ATHENS • TOKYO • MILAN
MADRID • WARSAW • BUDAPEST • AUCKLAND

One last time, for Ed,
whose legacy of love lives in my heart

Published August 1992

ISBN 0-373-31180-X

A COVENTRY COURTSHIP

Printed in U.S.A.

"Those dear girls must regain their place in Society."

Udora infused her voice with conviction.

"Dear girls, my eyes! The three of them are hell cats and well you know it." Bently had to admit to enjoying raising her ire.

"Guard your tongue, sir. Remember your position!" she shot back in some little heat.

Bently leaned into his seat never once removing his gaze from Udora's face. Fascinating! he thought.

"Forgive me, my lady," he said, "*if* I have spoken out of turn. From this moment forward, your every wish is my command."

"And that is as it should be, is it not?" Udora replied smugly.

We shall see about that, thought Bently, even as he agreed.

Books by Phyllis Taylor Pianka

HARLEQUIN REGENCY ROMANCE

MIDNIGHT FOLLY
DAME FORTUNE'S FANCY
3–THE TART SHOPPE
34–THE CALICO COUNTESS
48–THE LARK'S NEST

HARLEQUIN INTRIGUE

16–MIDSUMMER MADNESS

PROLOGUE

THE LAMPLIGHTER had long since completed his rounds in St. John's Wood, when the messenger arrived at The Lark's Nest that foggy evening. The house was lit from cellar to attic and he silently cursed his employer for insisting that the message be delivered post haste.

The sound of singing accompanied by a lute drifted through an open window. The woman's voice was as clear and lilting as the nightingale's song on an April morn. It could only be Yvette, the Lark from Lyons. The escaped French aristocrat, now Lady Bancroft, who had rocked all of London with scandal a year or so back.

Udora Middlesworth was one of those fortunate enough to be situated in the centre of the salon where Lord and Lady Bancroft were the evening's singular attraction. Udora gazed at them fondly. And why shouldn't she share the limelight? It was thanks to her that they had found each other.

Less than two years ago, Yvette had been posing as a housemaid at the Berrington estate, and now she had assumed her rightful place in Society as the wife of Lord Bancroft. Udora twisted a coil of copper-coloured hair around her finger as she gazed at the adoring couple and then up at her own fiancé.

She smiled and squeezed Charles's hand. And in a few months she would be saying her own vows to this handsome man. Charles was such a pet. He was, in truth, a bit stuffy at times but she would see to it that he lost some of his starch. A well-seasoned man required a generous measure of spice...at least to please her palate. And if nothing else, she knew how to train a husband. After all, this was to be her fifth marriage in eleven years. The fact that Charles was a few years her junior boded well that this time her husband might outlive her.

She laughed aloud at the irony of the implications. Charles looked down at her, one eyebrow raised in question. She smiled and shook her head. "It's nothing, my love. I was just thinking about all that has transpired in the past few months."

He patted her hand. "It makes one believe in miracles."

Miracles, indeed, thought Udora. Men were so charmingly naive. Didn't they realize that it was the women who chose them and not the other way round? The only miracle was that now nothing on earth could keep them from their mutual destiny...once she had decided what it was to be. She sighed happily.

At that moment the butler approached with the silver salver bearing the urgent summons to Coventry for the reading of the Thackery will.

CHAPTER ONE

IT WAS THREE DAYS LATER before Udora had her affairs in order so that she could make her departure for Coventry with a clear conscience. Her abigail, Maggie McGee, would accompany her, leaving the McMasters in charge of The Lark's Nest. Charles insisted that he be permitted to escort her in his elegant barouche complete with outriders and liveried attendants. Udora was impressed. Her own carriage was quite adequate but it would be ever so much more interesting to make her entrance in splendour. To give him credit, Udora admitted, Charles was the perfect gentleman, always solicitous of her comfort as well as her reputation. When the journey extended into latc afternoon, he ordered the carriage to stop at a country inn for a pleasing repast of tea and currant tarts topped with rich clotted cream.

Udora looked about the comfortable and surprisingly clean common-room. "What a lovely inn, Charles. Are we to spend the night here?"

His face suffused with colour. "Oh, I think not, my dear. We could hardly risk compromising your reputation. I've sent a messenger on to Sir Clarence Clifford, advising him that we will be travelling through. They will have rooms prepared for us."

Udora wrinkled her nose. "I'd far sooner risk my reputation than my hearing. You know of course that we'll be required to spend the evening listening to the Clifford children inflict torture upon the violin and pianoforte? The inn would be a far better choice."

"I know you speak in jest, Udora. But now that we are betrothed, you must understand that the rules of Polite Society are not to be flouted."

Maggie, Udora's abigail and companion, gave an unladylike snort but one quelling look from Udora silenced her. Udora patted Charles's hand. "As you wish, my pet, but do let's find other accommodations on our return to London."

Charles smiled indulgently. "Certainly, if you like. We'll just collect your inheritance and be on our way back to Town. Speaking of your inheritance, have you any idea what the value of the Thackery jewels might be?"

"No idea at all. Harvey was only a half brother to Quentin Thackery. During the two years I was married to Harvey we never visited his family in Coventry. That's one reason I am so shocked to be named as beneficiary."

Charles flicked a bit of lint from his coat. "Whatever the value, the gems will look well on you."

Udora dimpled. "It is my intention to sell them. Then perhaps we might consider buying our own house."

"Nonsense, my dear. My mother is already having the east wing renovated. It's not a question of money, you know. I can well afford a house."

"Then what is it? Why must we live with your family?" She toyed with her beaded reticule. "You must know that a bird too long in the nest will soon lose its ability to fly."

Charles glanced at Maggie, then shot Udora a warning look. "This is not the time to discuss it, Udora."

Udora had a feeling that the time might never arrive.

As expected, the Cliffords made their guests welcome. With the children visiting their grandparents in Manchester, the interlude proved to be bearable but certainly not stimulating. The Cliffords were apparently cut from the same dull cloth as Charles's parents. It was well into the morning of the next day before Charles gave the signal to take their leave. As the barouche negotiated the narrow country roads, Udora felt as if she were able to breathe for the first time in hours.

Warwickshire was like many other countrysides. Gently rolling hills were criss-crossed with hedgerows and dotted with thatched-roof cottages and the occasional manor-house in varying degrees of grandeur. At last they reached a narrow road which Charles declared bordered the perimeter of the Thackery lands.

They had no more than crossed the intersection when a smart-looking gig drew up alongside them, hesitated for a moment, then leaped forward as the driver flicked a whip in the air. The snap caused Charles's horses to bolt, but his driver quickly brought them under control.

Udora had caught a clear glimpse of the gig's sole occupant: a dark-haired man wearing a many-caped cloak. There was a certain rugged appeal about his sun-bronzed face. But it was his eyes which had seemed to impale her for that brief moment, with a ruthless intensity which had caused her to catch her breath.

Charles swore competently, then apologized. "The fool. He might have killed us."

"I—I don't think so," Udora said. "Look, he's slowing down as if he's waiting for us." She laughed shakily. "I think he wants to race." She leaned forward, hands clasped in eager anticipation. "Let's have a go, Charles."

He gave her a scathing look. "Really, Udora. You'll get us killed even before you collect your inheritance. It is far better to ignore such rabble than to encourage them."

Udora sighed and leaned back. Clearly there was to be no discussion of the matter, which left her feeling rather like a kite which had lost the wind. As if the smug smile on her abigail's face wasn't enough, Charles reached forward and patted Udora's hand in much the same way he would comfort a child. She chose to ignore him. Her attention was still drawn to the man in the gig. After a moment or two he gave his horse the office and the two-wheeled carriage sped forward in a cloud of dust.

Charles feigned a cough. "There, you see, my love? The ruffian has taken it on the hoof."

"Yes, so I see," Udora said as the gig disappeared round a bend in the road. The disappointment in her voice was plainly heard as she settled back against the squabs. *A ruffian he might be,* she thought, *but he has shoulders to put the captain of the King's Guards to shame.*

The oppressive silence in the carriage directed their attention to the passing landscape. A wide ribbon of silver water wended through brakes and briers and copses of oak and beech. A flock of sheep heavy with wool grazed contentedly at the verge alongside the road where a young shepherd boy threw stones at a huge crow perched atop a linden tree. He waved as the barouche rattled by, then slowed as the horses approached a narrow stone bridge. Udora returned the boy's wave until Charles gave her a speaking look.

A scant two miles beyond the bridge the carriage slowed again to pass through a stone gateway marked with a nondescript sign which read Amberleigh. Udora tensed. This was it. They were here.

Just as they rounded a turn in the lane the house appeared in front of them, wings spread wide like some fanciful bird of prey. "But this can't be the Thackery place," Udora declared. "I expected a cottage, not a country estate." It was a large house; stucco and stone, with arched windows on the first floor, on which was centred a huge, circular portico extending upward in a set-back to the second floor. A large, stained glass dome topped the portico with the pattern repeated in balance atop the towers on each of the two wings. The afternoon sunlight sifting through tall cedar trees touched the leaded glass domes with tongues of golden fire.

"Amberleigh," Udora whispered. "Now I know where the name comes from."

Maggie shuddered. "Aye, and it's spooky, ma'am. Maybe even haunted, like."

"Nonsense. It's the trees and the undergrowth which make the house seem oppressive. They need to be trimmed. I'm afraid the place is in a sad state of neglect."

Charles looked suddenly gloomy. "Looks gone to seed, I'd say. I hope they've taken better care of the stables."

No one commented further until the carriage rolled to a halt on the gravel drive in front of the portico steps. The driver leaped down from his perch and trotted round to help them alight.

Charles grumbled. "Not so much as a butler or footman to attend us."

It was, in fact, the gaunt-looking housekeeper who met them at the door. Her white hair was pulled back in a severe knot at the back of her head, causing her skin to stretch shiny-tight and her eyes to all but disappear into narrow slits. "*Guten tag,* your ladyship. I am Frau Kragen." Her voice was surprisingly strong, considering her lean frame. She smoothed an immaculate apron and stepped aside to permit their entry. "Please come in. Herr Vatley vaits for you in ze library."

Dorrance Watley, a rotund little man with a pleasantly bland face, rose from his chair as the library door opened. When the housekeeper announced them and they entered, he looked puzzled. "Udora Thackery Middlesworth?" he asked, chins wobbling.

She dimpled. "Udora Benson Hendricks Thackery Kinkaid Middlesworth, to be precise."

His jaw dropped like an unlatched window. "My lady, forgive me. I didn't realize . . . I expected someone much older than yourself."

She laughed. "I'll take that as a compliment. I hope we haven't kept you waiting too long, Mr. Watley. The drive from London took rather longer than we planned."

"Not at all, my lady. Please be seated." He turned to the housekeeper. "I believe you were going to serve refreshments?" She left looking somewhat disgruntled at having to miss the proceedings. Mr. Watley settled them into comfortable chairs, then took his place behind the desk. They spoke of pleasantries until Mrs. Kragen arrived with the tea tray.

The refreshments consisted of thin squares of buttered bread, filled with paper-thin slices of Westphalian ham and slivers of a pale yellow cheese. Fancy cakes and apple tarts were arranged on a cut-glass plate the shape of a five-pointed star.

Charles merely picked at his food, but Udora noticed that Dorrance Watley ate well. When he at last finished, the solicitor looked pointedly at Charles. "Would the gentleman prefer to wait in the drawing room?"

Charles scowled. "The gentleman would prefer to remain with her ladyship."

Udora nodded and Mr. Watley clamped his fingers over his round belly and settled his chin into the folds of his neck. "Now then, to business. I assume you would prefer to dispense with the reading of the entire will and to go right to the section which applies directly to you?"

Udora dimpled. "Whatever you think is best."

Charles leaned forward to rest his forearms on the desk. "A capital idea. We expect to start back for London as soon as the papers are signed."

Watley jiggled his chins as a smile split his face. "Oh, I hardly think that would be possible."

Charles looked contentious. "And pray why not?"

"Perhaps you had best wait until you hear the contents of his lordship's last will and testament."

"Then do get on with it."

Watley chuckled softly as if in response to some private whimsy. "Ahem," he said, flipping through the pages of paper. "Here, I believe is the section pertaining to you, my lady." He adjusted his spectacles to sit at the end of his nose. "'And to Lady Udora Middlesworth, beloved widow of my half brother, Harvey Thackery, I bequeath into her tender and loving care, my most precious possessions, the Thackery Jewels.'"

Charles coughed and looked over at Udora, his face beaming. She blinked at him, too surprised by the unexpected expression of affection from a relation she had never met to offer more than a weak smile. Still, she conceded, quickly gathering her wits about her, Quentin Thackery, God rest his soul, wouldn't be the first man to have worshipped her from afar. But how kind of him to have remembered her in his will. She saw that Watley was awaiting their full attention and she nodded her head in what she hoped was a regal gesture befitting this most recent acquisition.

Watley was hard put to suppress a grin. He continued. "'Because of her devoted and loving care of my sainted half brother during the time of his illness preceding his death, I entrust to Udora Thackery Middlesworth the guardianship of my beloved twin daughters, Emerald and Amethyst, and my precious adopted daughter, Topaz. The guardianship shall continue until the girls marry or until such time as they reach their majority.'"

Udora jumped up. "What? What are you saying?"

Watley considered her question with a cool look of amusement. "Why, I thought it was rather plainly put, my lady. His lordship has granted you the privilege of rearing his children. A high honour, I assure you, knowing how Quentin Thackery doted on his three girls."

Charles had turned pale as the underside of a fresh-caught flounder. "But...but what of the Thackery Jewels?"

"Jewels? Why, my good fellow. I thought you understood. The jewels are the girls themselves. Emerald, Amethyst and Topaz. Clever, isn't it?"

Udora sank back onto the chair. Pistachions! She should have known things had been going all too well this past year. Now Dame Fortune had taken it upon herself to turn the wine into vinegar.

To say that Udora and Charles were stunned was as if to say that Prinny was a trifle overweight.

Udora required several deep breaths before she was able to speak. "Before we...uh...proceed any further, Mr. Watley, I must protest. Surely there is some mistake. Lord Leighton must have either misspoke himself or have become legally incompetent. I was not meant to be a mother. I know nothing about feeding and cleaning one child, to say nothing of three." She hesitated. "Moreover, I confess to being quite at odds with children to the point where I would perhaps do more harm to them than good."

His gaze impaled her. "Quentin Thackery, Lord Leighton was quite sane. Is it that you dislike children, my lady?"

She shifted uncomfortably. "*Dislike* is a rather strong word, though as I think on it, I do recall my third husband's four nephews who were obnoxious little..." She left the invective hanging in the air. "The fact of the matter is that I am about to become a bride once again and there is simply no place in my life for the added responsibility of three children."

She patted Charles's knee. "Mr. Willingsly and I thought to tour the Continent for six months or so, then perhaps take passage on a packet to the Indies. They say the climate is glorious there. All sun and balmy breezes."

Watley was not to be distracted. He gripped the front of his waistcoat. "Indeed. If I may continue, there is yet another clause. In essence, it states that as guardian of the children you will have complete control over them and their immediate futures. In addition, you will be responsible for the running of the estate, until such time as the girls marry or reach their majority. You will, of course, be compensated."

"Compensation is not the issue," she snapped.

Watley's disdainful expression was replaced by a look of grudging respect. "I have every confidence that you will change your mind, my lady."

Charles crossed his legs and flicked a piece of lint from his nankeens. "I have the strangest feeling that we've missed something here. It occurs to me, Mr. Watley, that you have not told us very much about these children."

"Ahem. That, sir, was not entirely an oversight. I thought it better to let you form your own opinions."

Udora tugged on the strings of her reticule. "I find that less than reassuring. Perhaps you should begin by telling us how old the girls are."

His face turned a faint shade of green. "Fifteen, my lady."

"Fifteen. Fifteen! You realize this puts them far beyond the age where they can still be moulded and shaped. Would the fifteen-year-old be the eldest?"

"They are all the same age, your ladyship. You see two of the girls are twins. The third girl is adopted but as it happens, she is older only by two months."

Udora looked appalled. "Tell me this is a bad dream brought on by a remnant of a tainted pork pie I dined on earlier today."

Watley leaned back and expanded his chest. "I think you'll find the girls quite spirited and rather attractive...." He added as if to qualify, "I mean, of course, attractive in their own way."

Charles tightened his lips, blew out a stream of air, then spoke caustically. "Just where are they, if I may be so bold? I assume they are away at school?"

"Not at school. I thought it best for us to spend some time alone before they made their presence known."

Udora rose and went to the window. Mr. Watley took the opportunity to speak in rather glowing terms about the estate.

"You will find Amberleigh consists of a working farm with the residence, parklands, gardens, stables, paddocks, the home farm and five tenant farms along with their cottages. It is run by the bailiff, a Mr. Dodson, who, although he is new to the position, seems to be doing a fairly decent job of it."

"And the hunting?" Charles asked.

"You'll not want for game, sir, should you find yourself spending time at the estate," he said, looking to Udora for her reaction.

Udora smiled and turned. "Where I go, Charles is sure to follow. However, Mr. Watley, I regret to say that I have no intention of accepting my, uh, inheritance. Surely the children have someone within the family who would be willing, indeed willing and eager to assume their guardianship."

Watley rested his elbows on the desk and leaned forward fixing her with his gaze. "There is no one, my lady. No one, save a maiden aunt who has gone to live in the colonies. His lordship left strict orders that she was to have naught to do with the rearing of the three children."

"Pity. Then what will happen to them?"

He spread his hands. "They will be treated as orphans and will become wards of the Crown."

"There must be another way."

"What do you suggest?"

Udora was silent, finding no reasonable response. At last she shuddered. "I detest the country."

Watley turned to Udora. "If I may make a suggestion, madam. I have made arrangements with the housekeeper for you to take up residence at the estate beginning this day. Would it not be prudent for you to meet the children before you decide to refuse their guardianship?"

Udora spoke gravely. "It wouldn't make the slightest difference, I assure you. And I wonder, would it not be unwise to raise their hopes?"

"Quite frankly, I don't know." He stood and came round the corner of his desk to loom over her. "But let me ask you this, Lady Udora. I am told that you are much admired as a woman with a keen spirit for adventure. Could you be content knowing that you had passed over an opportunity which might have significantly altered the direction of your life?"

Udora was silent. She didn't care for the direction her thoughts were taking, not to mention her life. If she weren't careful she might find herself stuck here in the country like a turnip waiting for a harvest which never came. She drew a deep breath as she returned to her seat next to Charles.

"Mr. Watley. Perhaps you would be good enough to summon the girls."

"Yes, yes, indeed." Dorrance Watley hurriedly waddled across the room to the bell pull. The housekeeper responded even before he resumed his seat. He eased his waistcoat across his generous stomach. "Will you kindly ask the girls to join us, Mrs. Kragen?"

Granite faced, she nodded and left the room.

"You must forgive Mrs. Kragen," Mr. Watley said. "She has been in sole charge of the girls for some time now."

"And would not take lightly to having someone usurp her position. Am I not correct?" Udora enquired.

"Ah, but my lady. That is why you are so perfect to assume the guardianship. Your reputation as a diplomat precedes you. You shall soon have the servants as well as the young ladies in the palm of your hand."

Udora gave him a quelling look. "Flattery does not serve you well, Mr. Watley."

Discomfited, he started to respond but was gratefully interrupted when the children were herded into the room by Mrs. Kragen.

It was all Udora could do to restrain a gasp. Never had she seen children so untidy. The one with silvery-white hair looked as if she had slept in a stable. The other two girls were identical, save that one had honey-coloured hair while the other girl's hair was a shade or so darker. To say they were unkempt was being overly charitable. All three stood like sticks in a snowbank.

Mrs. Kragen inclined her head towards Udora. "Your ladyship, may I present Miss Emerald, Miss Amethyst and Miss Topaz?" As they continued to stare sullenly at the company seated in the room, Mrs. Kragen hissed, "Your manners, girls. Curtsy to her ladyship."

Udora smiled gallantly, disguising her distaste for their state of dishabille. "Please, come sit down. Now I know that two of you are twins but I must say, you all rather, uh, resemble one another."

Mrs. Kragen jerked her head towards a settee. "Miss Emerald and Miss Amethyst are ze tvins. Miss Topaz is two months older."

Charles stared wide-eyed. "Surely you and Mr. Watley have had your little jest. Those simply cannot be their real names."

Miss Topaz darted her tongue across her bottom lip in an innocent yet sensual gesture. She contrived to look demure as a twelve-year-old, but there was something in the way she stared at Charles that made Udora sense trouble. "Our parents had a romantic sense of humour, sir. I am called Taz instead of Topaz."

"And my name is Em or Emmy," the honey-haired girl said. "Amy prefers Amy to Amethyst." Amy ducked her head and leaned against Emmy.

Udora inclined her head. "A fair exchange, I suppose. I've never been keen about my own name but there was little I could do with it."

Topaz nodded. "Yes, my lady. But you did manage to change your other name a few times, I believe."

Mrs. Kragen gasped. "Dat iss enough. Now go to your rooms und dress for tea."

Emmy feigned innocence. "But I thought we were already dressed, Mrs. Kragen."

Udora chuckled. They had spirit. Not unlike herself when she was fifteen. "If nothing else, you might want to brush your hair, my dears."

Amy looked grave. "Taz never brushes her hair."

"Of course she does," Udora said. "And such pretty hair it is, I'm sure. Like angel flax in the sun. Why not ask your abigail to help you arrange it in a becoming fashion before you come downstairs?"

Mrs. Kragen looked discommoded. "Go on vit you now. Shoo. Tell Dulcey to help."

They left the room without benefit of curtsy or nod, but Taz looked back over her shoulder. "You ought to know that Dulcey can't tell a hairbrush from a currycomb."

Before Mrs. Kragen had a chance to reply, the girls dashed from the room and scurried towards the stairs, all the while laughing and giggling like six-year-olds.

Udora slowly let out her breath. "Well, Mr. Watley. I can fully understand why you chose to say so little about the *children*."

He wiped his hand across his chin. "Ahem. They do seem to be a bit of a handful."

Charles looked nervous. "Anyone would be a fool to undertake their guardianship no matter how well they are provided for."

Mr. Watley hastened to reassure them. "One must not overlook the fact that they are already fifteen years of age. They could be married and off your hands in a year, two at the most."

Udora looked at him in amazement. "Pistachions! It takes a good deal more than a dowry to enter successfully into the Marriage Mart. No self-respecting mother would let her son within a country mile of one of these girls." She spread her hands in a final gesture. "Truly, Mr. Watley, I can't see that I have a thing to offer these girls."

His expression reminded her suddenly of a long-eared puppy who had lost his bone. "I'm begging you, your ladyship, don't be hasty in your decision. Remain here at the house for a week. It can do no harm and it might prevent you from making a mistake you will regret for the rest of your life."

Charles had been gazing off at the distant hedgerows when a covey of pheasants flushed from a bramble bush caught his eye. Although everything else had gone awry, the hunting might prove to be superb. He looked at Udora. "We've come this far, my dear. I think we could contrive to stay on for the week. There can be no real harm in in."

"I suppose we won't know that to be true or not unless we stay on." She sighed. "Very well, Mr. Watley. A week, no more. And I make no other promise."

He hooked his thumbs in his waistcoat and chuckled. "A wise decision, my lady. One I'm sure you will one day be grateful you made."

"I only wish I could believe you."

CHAPTER TWO

AFTER UDORA and Charles saw Mr. Watley to the door, Mrs. Kragen led them up the wide staircase to the next floor. "The *kinder* also have rooms in this ving, my lady." She looked back over her shoulder with a guarded expression. "Ve don't use ze vest ving because of our limited staff. I haff giffen you the Amber Suite but if you vish another..." she said, opening the door.

Udora surveyed the comfortably appointed room lit in part by an amber domed window directly over the bed. "But it's charming. Why wouldn't I want it?"

"There are those who are afraid here at *nacht*."

Udora looked first at Charles, whose eyes danced with high good humour, and then back at Mrs. Kragen. "Indeed, and why is that?"

"The rustlings, my lady. They come in the dead of *nacht* through the walls and near the fireplace."

Charles laughed. "Are you suggesting the room is haunted?"

"Ach, 'tis not for me to say. But if her ladyship vishes, I vould give her ze oval suite."

Udora laid her shawl on the bed. "Don't fret, Mrs. Kragen. I am not the least bit afraid of noises in the night. I assure you I will be quite comfortable in this lovely room."

Mrs. Kragen gave her a skeptical look and bustled across the pale blue Oriental carpet to open a door to an adjoining room. "Und your maid vill sleep here."

"Very well, and what about Mr. Willingsly? What room will he be given?"

"If you vill come vit me, sir, I vill show you to your room down the hall." At the doorway she turned to look back. "Mr. Coombs vill fetch your bags in a few moments, my lady, und zupper vill be served at six."

Charles made a face at Udora over the top of Mrs. Kragen's head. "Rather early, wouldn't you say?"

Udora smiled back at him. "They dine early in the country, my pet. Shall we meet in the library at half past five for sherry?"

He bowed. "Best offer I've had all day, my love. While you nap I think I'll have a look at the prads."

"Oh, I couldn't begin to sleep." Udora had a sudden thought. "I wonder, Mrs. Kragen, would there be a gig in the stable? I'd rather enjoy driving round the grounds before I dress for dinner."

"*Ja*, my lady. I vill tell Blodgett, him being the stablemaster, to harness the horse and bring it round to the front."

Charles blustered. "You surely don't intend to go without benefit of escort."

"Don't be so stuffy, Charles. This is not London. I am comfortable driving a gig and I'm sure I shall be quite safe. Is that not so, Mrs. Kragen?"

She shrugged. "*Ja*. Zere are rumours, of course, of things happening, but I haff never known zem to be true."

Udora chuckled. "I am quite willing to take my chances."

Charles muttered something best not heard and motioned Mrs. Kragen to lead on.

Maggie had already begun to explore the armoires and chests in the two rooms. She sniffed. "Drawer linin's not been changed in an age. Musty, too." She flopped down on the narrow bed in her smaller room. "Aye, but the mattress is good and it smells of lavender. Reckon it's one of them featherbeds." She rose and came back into Udora's room, then shivered and stopped.

"Saints above! The housekeeper was right, my lady. There *is* something about this room that raises the goose flesh on my arms."

"Nonsense. It's far too pleasant a room for anything of that nature. Why, just look how the sunlight filters through the amber glass, sending such a pretty glow."

Maggie's shoe-button eyes nearly popped out. "Then wot was that noise, my lady? It sounded like footsteps in the wall over by the fireplace. I never once heard o' sunlight wot wears 'obnail boots."

Udora listened but the footsteps had ceased. "It's nothing, I'm sure," she said. "You know how these old houses are. Sounds echo and boards creak. Even The Lark's Nest had its peculiar noises."

"But none the likes o' these."

There was a soft repeated tapping and both women jumped. Udora inched open the door, then laughed as she looked into the hallway. "There, you see? It's only Mr. Coombs come to bring our valises." She opened the door farther to allow the white-haired servant unobstructed entry.

"Just place them near the armoire, Mr. Coombs. My abigail can manage from there."

He mumbled a "Yes, ma'am" and bobbed his head. At least Udora thought he did, but she realized when he left the room and closed the door behind him that his head was in a constant state of movement.

Maggie had also noticed the servant's bobbing head and raised her eyes to the ceiling. "I'll wager a month's earning that 'e's seventy if 'e's a day. Gone to seed like the rest o' this place."

Udora sighed. "You're beginning to sound like Charles."

"Maybe so, m'lady, but I might have the right of it. And I don't fancy stayin' on me own in this here room, whilst you goes off in the gig."

"Then come along if you wish."

"Mind you, if we was *both* to stay 'ere, I expect a nap for you and me would be just the thing," Maggie said hopefully.

Udora shook her head. "I couldn't nap just now. In truth, Maggie, I'm quite mystified by my own eagerness to see the rest of the Thackery holdings. I might even call on the bailiff to ask him to show me about."

Maggie was less than pleased, but she managed to keep her grumbles to a minimum while she assisted her mistress out of her travelling dress and into a costume suitable for a country drive.

Later, as Udora and Maggie were tooling along in the gig down the narrow track which bordered the hedgerows, Udora sighed. "Well, this is a far cry from Regent's Park, but the air is rather nice."

Maggie sniffed. "Iffen you like the smell o' the stable, it is."

Udora laughed. "I do detect a rather ripe odour at times, but I daresay that the streets of London smell far worse just before a rainstorm clears the sewers. At least we don't have to worry about thieves and cut-purses here in the country."

Maggie pointed to a hill some distance away. "Then wot's 'e doing up there on 'is 'orse? 'E's been watchin' us since we left the hedgerows."

Udora leaned forward for a closer look. The black-cloaked rider sat motionless upon his dark mount. Silhouetted against the late afternoon sun he called to mind a menacing figure from some half-forgotten nightmare. The first faint swirls of mist beginning to collect on the verge added to the ghostly effect. Udora shuddered in spite of herself.

She drew back on the reins and the mare slowed to a walk. A second look at the apparition tended to reassure her. He sat his horse like a general reviewing his troops. Though his face was in shadow, there was something rather familiar about his silhouette.

She caught her breath. "Oh, dear, isn't he the fellow who overtook our carriage earlier today and challenged us to race?"

"Aye, 'e is that. And a devil into the bargain, mark my words," Maggie whispered, making the sign of the cross.

"Nonsense. He is nothing more extraordinary than a man on a horse though I confess I have no idea what his intentions might be."

His black stallion snorted and pawed the ground with increasing impatience. Udora sat quite quietly. Although the sun still lit the tops of the trees, oddly, there was no one working the fields. The two women were alone and completely at his mercy, should he choose to accost them. Strangely enough, Udora sensed no fear. She nudged her horse into a trot. In the distance ahead she saw a spiral of smoke rising from a cottage chimney. That would be the bailiff's cottage, she surmised. She slapped the reins and clicked her tongue to urge the mare to greater speed, but the nag flattened her ears and refused more than a token trot.

It was enough, apparently, to spur the watcher on the knoll into action. He tapped his heels against his horse's flanks and as his stallion picked its way through the low-growing gorse, dirt and dust scattered on the wind.

"Lord o' mercy, 'e's comin' after us," Maggie screeched. "'E's goin' to get us."

"Not if I have my way about it," Udora said, cracking the whip in the air over the mare's back. The sound was like a shot above the clatter of hooves on the hard-packed road. Unfortunately the mare had a mind of her own because she was not to be hurried.

Maggie clung to the side of the gig, her bonnet askew, her shoe-button eyes dark with fear. "Mother of God. It's too late. We'll niver get away."

"Don't be a twit," Udora said with more courage than she thought she had. "He won't lay hands on us. Not as long as I have the whip."

The rider was fast approaching. In a moment he was alongside them and reaching for the horse's bridle in order to pull it up. The mare needed no urging. She jerked to a stop, her eyes wide, nostrils flaring, her ears laid back against her head.

Udora knotted the reins in the ring and grabbed the whip, brandishing it with both hands like a sword. "Stay back. I warn you, if you touch one hair of our heads, I'll see to it that you may no longer enjoy the pleasures of a complete man."

The rider pivoted in the saddle until he was facing her. "Now why would I want to touch you, madam?"

Udora was taken aback. Whether it was the softly menacing tone of his voice or the unexpected flash of anger in his dark brown eyes, she was left nearly speechless. Her breathing was shallow and her hands began to shake. The fact that she was unable to control either made her furious.

"Really! You unprincipled ruffian. What do you mean by pulling us up like that? You might have killed us."

"An unlikely possibility, madam. Quite the reverse, I'd say. You might well have killed the mare, or maimed her at the very least."

"I beg your pardon?

"It is not my pardon, you must beg, madam, but that of the poor horse who is about to go lame. Another mile or so and she may have fallen, causing her permanent injury. Have you no consideration for her? Can't you see that she has thrown a shoe?"

Maggie sat straighter and primped her hair. "Then you ain't goin' to attack us?" She sounded somewhat disappointed.

Udora raised her eyes to the heavens but not before she caught the look of amusement which crossed the rider's face. The bronzed skin at the corners of his eyes wrinkled and his moustache twitched in a most delightful way.

He touched two fingers to his forehead in the semblance of a salute. "I apologize if I frightened you, miss."

Maggie batted her eyelashes. "Oh, it t'weren't me I was 'fraid fer. 'Twas 'er ladyship I was thinkin' of."

"Of course. I should have known."

He turned to Udora. "Would you mind terribly lowering the whip? My horse is apt to bolt."

He inclined his head and doffed his cap. "My name is Aaron Bently."

Udora was affronted by his willingness to introduce himself to her without benefit of a third party, but this was, after all, the country. One must learn to make allowances. She looked pointedly at Maggie who stopped gaping long enough to perform the necessary introduction.

"May I present my mistress, Lady Udora Middlesworth. And *I* am Maggie McGee, recently from London," she added with a touch of hauteur.

The man named Bently looked solemn. "Ah, then, my lady. It must be yourself who has inherited the Thackery brood along with control of this sadly neglected estate."

"News certainly travels quickly in the country. If truth be told, I have yet to come to a decision. It is a rather large responsibility for a woman in my circumstances."

"Indeed. A large responsibility for anyone. May I assume then you are a maiden lady?"

Maggie giggled until Udora silenced her with a scathing look. "A widow, if you must know." She regarded him cooly. "Tell me, does one always engage in such personal conversations here in the middle of a country lane?"

He smiled. "Only when one is about to become a neighbour. I live at Partridge Run, the estate bordering Amberleigh on the north."

"How interesting," she said, with considerable lack of sincerity. She studied his well-worn fustians and the boots that were caked with mud and what else she dared not imagine. "May I assume then that you are the bailiff at Partridge Run?" she asked, mocking his own method of intimate questioning.

He laughed. "It is true, I manage the holdings."

"Very good. Perhaps you can point me in the direction of my own bailiff's cottage. I would like to introduce myself to him before the day escapes me." She noticed too late that she had used the possessive. He noticed it, too.

He tried unsuccessfully to hide a smile as he backed his mount away from the gig and donned his cap. "If you will be so good as to follow me, your ladyship, perhaps we can persuade the man to see to your mare. Until then, I suggest that you walk the horse at a gentle pace."

Udora sniffed and gathered the reins in her gloved hand. "I shall do that, providing you promise never again to swoop down on us like some dark avenging angel."

The bailiff gave her a wry look and appeared to be about to speak. Instead, he flicked the reins and rode off ahead of them at a slow trot.

Maggie leaned back against the seat and fanned her face with her hand. "Lawks, m'lady. 'E is somethin' else, now ain't 'e?"

"I'm sure I don't know what you mean. He is an arrogant brute, I'll certainly vouch for that."

"Aye, with the eyes of a devil and the smile of a saint. I wouldn't mind the likes 'o him chasin' after me in the dark."

"Be careful, Maggie. Your imagination is sure to land you in the briers someday."

"Yes, ma'am, I'll remember that. But 'e was one fine lookin' gent." She glanced covertly out from beneath her bonnet. "I could 'a' sworn that you were lookin' 'im over the same way you looked over Mr. Willingsly the first time 'e came to call at The Lark's Nest."

"Pistachions! To compare Charles with this . . . this clodhopper is like comparing a fine painting to a child's first scribbles on a slate."

"Yes, ma'am. Whatever you say."

Udora pointedly ignored her abigail's smirk. There were certain disadvantages in keeping a servant too long in one's employ. She sighed. Ah, yes, the girl was impudent and outspoken but she was skilled with both the needle and the curling tongs and most of the time was quite good company. Besides, Udora could not abide servility and preferred honesty, even in a servant. That alone saved Maggie from getting the sack.

It was with some relief that Udora watched the man named Bently turn into the short lane and dismount in front of a stone house with shrubs grown nearly to the top of the windows. She drew the gig alongside and waited while Bently tied her horse to a post and came to assist her down from the gig.

She frowned. "This is the bailiff's house? I would have thought he would have taken more pride in its appearance."

Bently grunted. "I rather suspect the gentleman has more pressing concerns."

"Such as?" she asked, closing her parasol with a snap.

"I think that would be better left for Mr. Dodson to tell you himself. Would you like me to accompany you?"

"If you wish. You seem to know the man. I always find it helpful to have a proper introduction."

Bently gave her a quizzical look and she regarded him with cool disdain, quite unable to resist giving him a proper set-down. "I realize that the customs in the country differ somewhat from those of the city, Mr. Bently, but when the amenities are carefully observed, the quality of life can only prosper."

One look at Maggie's silly grin served to remind Udora that her abagail remembered only too well the countless times Udora had cast the amenities aside in order to manoeuvre and manipulate a situation to her own advantage.

Udora gave her a speaking look and handed Maggie her parasol. "You will remain in the gig until our business is finished." Maggie sat down with a flounce. *Yes, some discipline was definitely in order. The girl would be pouting when they returned. Ah, well. It served her right.*

Udora smiled up at the bailiff. "Mr. Bently, if you will lead the way."

Aaron Bently nodded curtly and stepped ahead of her to the front door where he banged the knocker three times. It was then that Udora noticed his considerable limp. She found herself wondering how it came about. A fall from a horse? An accident of birth? Whatever the cause, the injury didn't seem to hamper him. How fortunate that he was a country man instead of a London dandy. A limp would have been a decided disadvantage for a man caught up in the giddy social whirl of the Season.

He turned towards her. "There doesn't seem to be an answer. Shall I open the door, my lady?"

"Yes, do. I believe I see someone sleeping in the chair. Perhaps he is ill."

"Very well. You had best wait outside."

"Nonsense." She pushed him aside and strode past him. "Great heavens! What is that awful stench? I could swear it is Blue Ruin."

"I believe it is, my lady. The fellow seems to be well into his cups." Aaron Bently walked over to the chair where the brown-haired, bewhiskered man was half lying, half sitting with an empty bottle in his hand. Two more lay on the floor near his muddy boots. Bently shook him roughly. "Wake up, Dodson. Pull out of it, man, you have company."

Dodson stared up at them bleary-eyed, swore competently, then fell back into a state of unconsciousness.

Bently straightened. "I'm afraid it's no use."

"Does this happen often?"

"Need you ask? All you have to do is look around you at the sad state of the farm."

Udora was surprised by Bently's forthrightness, but she could not deny the truth of his statement. She nodded. "He hardly seems a good choice for a bailiff. I wonder how Lord Leighton came to hire him."

"Dodson came to Amberleigh only three years ago. The previous bailiff was an old family retainer but he unfortunately passed on to his maker. Dodson is something of a wastrel who should have been got rid of long ago but there was only the law firm left in charge of the estate and they are too far removed to know what is going on."

"Yes. I can see how that might be. Well, there's nothing to be done here. Shall we go?"

They went out and closed the door behind them. Udora looked at her forlorn mare. "Now what am I to do about my lame horse? I don't suppose there is a stable near to hand?"

"Fortunately, there is. The previous bailiff was keen on horses and kept a stable on his property. However, it will take some time to shoe her and repair the damage. If you don't mind a tight squeeze, I'll take your horse to the stable in the back and harness my mount onto the gig to escort you home."

"I fear it would be a dreadful imposition." Udora laughed. "I didn't mean the squeeze. I only mean that you have already been most kind."

Bently smiled at her for he always admired a woman with wit. There was, in fact, much to admire about this woman with her china-blue eyes and radiant copper-coloured curls. But why Quentin Thackery had chosen her to take over the estate along with the Thackery children was too much for him to fathom. Putting this Society woman in charge of this run-down farm, not to mention those three mischief-makers would be like sending a rabbit into a den of foxes. He stole a glance at her well-turned ankle. At the very least Quentin Thackery knew a good-looking woman when he saw one. Unfortunately, her looks wouldn't trim the wick here in the country.

Udora, sensing his close scrutiny, touched her cheek with a gloved hand in a deliberately coquettish gesture, then mentally chastised herself for flirting with a man of low birth. To correct her lack of judgement, she hardened her voice. "I do regret taking you away from your duties, Mr. Bently. Surely the owner of Partridge Run is expecting you to return to look after his own interests."

He stroked his moustache in an effort to hide his merriment. "I admit the owner expects a great deal of his workers but he is most understanding. If you will permit me?" He walked over to the gig and began to unhitch the mare. Moments later he had taken the horse to the stable and returned.

"There is only the stable boy in charge this morning. He promises to have the smithy see to the horse and return it to you by nightfall. If you ladies are ready, I'll drive you home."

It *was* going to be a tight squeeze. Udora had thought to take the middle seat, but somehow Maggie contrived to place herself next to Bently. Udora wondered only for a moment if the choice had been deliberate. Then one look at Maggie's gleeful smile confirmed that it certainly had been.

Pistachions! she thought to herself, only to question why she felt so keenly disappointed. She made the mistake of looking up into Bently's face and the flicker of comprehension in his eyes caused her own face to turn pink with embarrassment.

Devil take the man. He had no right to be amused at her expense. No right at all.

As they tooled along the lane at a fairly brisk pace, Aaron Bently pointed out the natural beauty of the land. "The river is full this time of the year. Later in the summer one can almost walk across to that small wooded island. Some of the tenants fish for perch to help feed their families."

"And does the boundary of our land extend to the other side of the river?"

"The line falls down the middle. The workers you see cutting willows on the far side of the river belong to Partridge Run. The willow whips will be harvested and the women will weave them into baskets to be sold at market."

"They seem to be quite industrious. Why is there no one working in the fields at Amberleigh?"

"Lack of supervision, I'd say. The soil is good, and there is much to be done."

"Then it would appear that the first thing the new owner must do would be to replace Dodson."

"A wise decision, my lady."

"Oh, I wasn't referring to myself. I have no intention of staying on here. I was merely speaking in theory."

Bently nodded. "Of course, I quite understand. It would be foolish for you to take on such an extraordinary task. To oversee the running of the estate, along with trying to bring some order into the household, would be far beyond the capabilities of a woman, not to mention a woman as inexperienced as you."

Maggie shot him a dark look and administered a discreet but sharp poke in the ribs. He gave a yelp.

Udora leaned forward to look at him. "Is something wrong?"

He carefully let out his breath. "Not that I was aware of." He looked pointedly at Maggie. "Are you uncomfortable, miss?"

"Nothing that gettin' back to London won't cure. Tellin' her ladyship that she can't do something is like 'oldin' a carrot in front of a 'orse."

"Nonsense!" Udora said. "You are simply repeating what my husband used to say."

Bently turned the gig into the lane leading up to the house. "Oh, yes. Harvey Thackery. A good man. I met him a few times years ago."

"Actually, I was referring to my first husband, Thurgood Hendricks."

"Ah! Then you are twice widowed. What a tragedy for one so young."

Maggie began to giggle and would surely have offered a more complete account of Udora's marital adventures had not the look in Udora's eyes warned her off.

She was grateful when they finally arrived. "Here we are, then. I can't thank you enough, Mr. Bently, for seeing us home. After you hand us down you may drive the gig behind the house to the stables and unhitch. Then if you wish, stop in the kitchen. Mrs. Kragen is sure to have a fresh pot of tea steeping."

His dark eyes held a glint of humour. "Thank you, your ladyship. I fear that duty calls and I must return to Partridge Run." He inclined his head, doffing his cap in an acceptable show of manners, then stepped down, being careful to favour his lame leg. "May I say what a pleasure it is to meet you, and you, Miss McGee."

Maggie puffed up her chest and tilted her head so that her hair swung becomingly. "The pleasure was *all* mine, Mr. Bently."

He smiled. "I wish you both a pleasant return journey to London."

"Oh, we ain't goin' for near a week yet."

"Indeed? Then perhaps we shall meet again."

Maggie batted her eyelashes. "I guess you knows where to find me." She looked embarrassed. "And 'er ladyship, o' course."

Udora shot her a dry look. "Come, Maggie. We mustn't delay Mr. Bently any longer." Udora swept up the front steps with Maggie trailing reluctantly behind her.

Maggie sighed with pure pleasure. "Now there's a man I could take a tumble for. Game leg and all."

"Don't be ridiculous. Mr. Bently is probably married with a pack of squalling brats to look after."

"Not him. He don't have that married look. I kin tell."

Udora didn't bother to argue. Although there was nothing about Aaron Bently that even remotely reminded Udora of the rakes in London, there was a certain something about him that bespoke bachelor. Somehow the knowledge brought a smile to her lips.

The smile was erased the minute she entered the main hall. When she saw the look on Charles's face, she took off her cloak and gave it to Maggie. "Take this upstairs, please. Then you may have a nap if you wish."

Maggie bobbed an acceptable curtsy with an unacceptable expression which said that she knew there was going to be fireworks the moment Udora and Charles were left alone.

CHAPTER THREE

CHARLES WAS practically prancing in his agitation. In truth, his posturing reminded her of a hot air balloon ready to burst. "Udora, I must speak to you at once." He studied her through his quizzing glass, a sure sign that he was thoroughly vexed.

Udora tried not to laugh at the affectation. "Really, Charles. May I not first refresh my toilette before we have a confrontation?"

It was as if he had not heard her. He took her arm and piloted her in the direction of the library. Udora chanced to look upward towards the landing where Maggie was unabashedly observing the entire scene and not trying in the least to disguise her distaste. Alas, Maggie made no secret of the fact that she held little respect for Charles Willingsly.

Once they were in the library, Charles motioned Udora to a chair. She sat down somewhat reluctantly but still maintained a playful air. "Really, Charles, is what you have to say so shattering that I might not be able to hear it standing up?"

"This is not a matter to be considered lightly, Udora. I am quite put off by what I've seen since we arrived here. The stables are a disgrace. There is not one decent mount in the lot, the stablemaster has been absent for nearly a fortnight, and as if that was not sufficient, one of the girls poured a bucket of swill on my breeches. I had to repair the damage without benefit of a valet."

He looked so outraged that Udora was forced to stifle her amusement. She reached for his hand and he took a seat alongside her. Her voice was soothing. "My dear, you've had a devilish day. Surely the girl didn't intend to spill the bucket onto your clothing."

"You think not? I'd venture to say she'd been planning it since the moment we arrived. We are not wanted here, Udora. Not by the girls, not by that sour housekeeper and not even by the stableboy who went so far as to suggest I see to my own horses. Can you credit that?"

"Appalling," she said in mock horror, but the sarcasm escaped him. She tilted her head. "Of course, Charles, it would seem that if he's the only one present to attend to the duties, that your horses might well benefit from your personal attention. However, I'll see if Mrs. Kragen knows of someone we can hire to look after them during the week that we remain here."

His face reddened. "Egad, Udora, don't tell me that you expect to stay on here."

"Only a week. I gave my word to Dorrance Watley."

"Then do not be surprised if you find that I have taken my departure, for I seriously doubt that I shall survive the night, much less seven days of these...these primitive accommodations."

He rose before she could respond and stalked from the room.

Udora remained seated in an effort to sort through her thoughts. He was not serious, of course. Charles wouldn't dream of leaving her alone in the country to fend for herself and Maggie. He was in a taking because his breeches had been soiled. Truth be told, he was always in a taking without his manservant present to supervise his wardrobe and keep it in repair.

And what would she do if he should insist that she return with him to London before the week was out? She immediately rejected the thought. He was too much the gentleman to force her to renege on her word. And he could be reasoned with if she struck the right chord. To be sure, there were certain discomforts to be endured, but at the same time, it was rather like an adventure. At the very least she must certainly remain in residence until a replacement was found for Dodson. The man was a drunkard. A liability to the farm and to three very impressionable young women.

For over an hour she sat wondering about the fate of the girls, then rose and climbed the stairs. Where were they now, and what sort of mischief were they getting up to? As if clairvoyant, they appeared at the door of their bedchamber in varying shades of brown and grey. It occurred to Udora that she was hard-pressed to remember ever seeing such unflattering gowns on anyone save a scullery maid in a country tavern.

"So there you are," she said. "How nice. I see you've changed into fresh dresses." Udora refused to comment on the fact that Topaz's hair remained unbrushed and that Amy was biting her nails. After all, she was not yet their guardian.

Topaz, looking almost ladylike with her hands tucked into the panniers of her skirt, stopped and waited next to an ornately carved chest. "We came to show you downstairs to the library."

Emerald, or was it Amethyst...glanced over at Taz and then back to Udora. "Yes, ma'am. It's so easy to lose your way in this house."

"How very kind of you. But first I must dress."

The other twin smiled sweetly. "We'll wait for you in your sitting-room."

Maggie was laying out Udora's gown when they reached her suite. Maggie had apparently taken it upon herself to choose the blue velvet with the gold braid at the bodice and hem. Matching slippers stood in wait beside a low chair and on the dressing table a blue and gold embossed fan lay next to an ivory lace handkerchief.

Udora was surprised. "I thought you were going to take a nap."

Maggie looked miffed. "With all the racket you made comin' and goin'?" She levelled her gaze at Udora. "And changing your mind as often as the clock changes time."

"I beg your pardon?"

"First ye tells me you'd be wearin' the brown satin tonight. So I lays it out and when I turns around it's back in the armoire. If it 'twas the blue you wanted you should ha' told me so from the start."

Perplexed, Udora chanced to look at the girls. Their poorly concealed grins gave mute testimony to their activities. She smiled in spite of herself.

"I'm sorry, Maggie. I should have said something before you went to the trouble of laying out the brown satin." Maggie mumbled something unintelligible, but it was the girls who drew Udora's attention. They were fidgeting and casting anxious looks amongst themselves.

"Girls, would you care to wait in my sitting room?" Udora asked.

They looked at one another then scurried into the next room, Taz leading the way.

Udora took Maggie by the shoulder and spoke softly. "Now what is this about the noises that kept you awake?"

"'Twas you when you was comin' and goin'... slammin' the drawers and knockin' your scent bottles about."

"But I..." Udora was about to protest that she had been nowhere near the room, but she thought better of it. Maggie was already looking a bit ragged. They were both distracted when one of the twins, Em, Udora thought, came back to stand in the doorway.

"It's very cold in here, Lady Udora. No one thought to light the fire. Come see."

"No need. I'll summon Dulcey." Udora started towards the bell pull but Em stayed her hand. "Please, Mrs. Kragen will be furious unless you first see for yourself."

Amy came to take Udora's other hand. Udora was happily surprised by the girls' attention. "Very well. Let's have a look. Perhaps Maggie can help us. She's quite capable."

Maggie humphed her disapproval but she obediently went to the mantle and felt along the marble. "There's no matches, my lady. How does they expect me to light a fire without matches?"

Taz picked up an ancient copy of *La Belle Assemblée* and pushed Maggie aside. "Oh, for goodness sake, let me." She passed the magazine in front of the fireplace once, and then once again as she spoke some strangely unintelligible words. In an instant the tinder burst into flames.

Maggie shrank back against the settee, her hands pressed to her cheeks. "Lord o' mercy. How did you do that?"

Taz tapped her fingers against her forehead. "It was nothing. But please don't ask me to do it again. I'm afraid the effort quite exhausts me. I must lie down." Em and Amy supported Taz on either side.

Then Em spoke. "She tires easily. I think it might be better if we waited for you in our own rooms. If you wish, Lady Udora, you may rap on our door when you are ready to go downstairs."

They were gone before either Udora or Maggie could compose herself, but their laughter could easily be heard as the girls ran down the hallway.

Maggie's shoe-button eyes were wide with terror. "'Eaven 'elp us. She's a witch, that one."

Udora leaned against the door frame, praying that she could regain her composure. "I . . . nonsense, Maggie. It was trickery. They are simply attempting to unsettle us. You know that as well as I." But the evidence was hard to dispute. The fire still burned brightly in the grate.

It was scarcely more than an hour when Udora knocked on the door to the girls' room and they assembled to take her down to the library. Maggie, having refused to stay alone, was given permission to accompany them.

Udora looked at Taz, who seemed filled to the brim with excitement. "It would appear that you are well rested, Miss Topaz. I beg your pardon. I mean, Taz."

Topaz fluttered her eyelashes. "I recover quickly."

They descended the stairs. Em, who was leading the way, turned sharply to the left as they reached the main floor. The other girls followed close behind her. Udora stopped.

"I thought the library was to the right."

"We know a more interesting way," Em said. "But of course if you're afraid..."

"Don't be silly. I trust you girls to take good care of Maggie and me."

Amy turned round and looked up at Udora. "Why would you trust us?"

Udora smiled and patted the girl's head. "Dear child, why wouldn't I?"

"Because..."

Taz stopped her with a look. "I think they really are afraid. Come on, then. We'll save it for another day." She made a turnabout and led the little party down the corridor in a more familiar direction.

Mrs. Kragen had just placed a tray of glasses on the oak table in the library and was pouring a sherry for Charles, who stood warming himself near the fire. She looked up.

"My lady, dinner vill be served in ze dining room at six o'clock. If your abigail vould like to join ze staff in ze kitchen, she is velcome."

Udora thanked her and nodded to Maggie, who appeared less than eager to leave, but did so, looking back but twice.

Charles, appearing more like himself in polished Hessians, tan breeches and a dark blue velvet dress coat, came over to kiss Udora's hand. He held it to his cheek for a moment and placed a kiss on her palm. "Forgive me, my love, for my ill temper this afternoon. I fear that I spoke in haste."

Udora was relieved. Perhaps the sherry had made him feel more magnanimous. Whatever it was, he was once again the fiancé whom she adored. She turned her hand to clasp his. "No apology is necessary, my pet. I can easily sympathize with your frustrations. You have been most patient under these trying circumstances."

"And you, my dear, are most understanding. Once we return to London and put all this behind us, we must proceed quickly with our wedding arrangements. I know Yvette and Andrew are planning a rout for us that will be the toast of the Season."

Udora, who loved parties and dancing more than anything in the world, was inexplicibly saddened. She turned away, pretending to examine a shelf of leather-bound books. "London seems so far away today."

"Only because you carry such a weight on your lovely shoulders."

"No. I think not, Charles." She didn't elaborate, for although she felt no burden, she could not clearly identify what she did feel. Instead she turned to the girls. "Taz, Em, Amy. Do you wish to partake of the apple cider?"

Taz sniffed. "Cider is for children. We always prefer the sherry. Isn't that right, Em, Amy?"

Eyes sparkling, they both nodded.

Udora, harkening back to her own misspent youth, suppressed a grin. "Oh, of course. Forgive me, I didn't realize that your tastes had become so sophisticated. Charles would you fill a glass for each girl?"

His eyebrows shot upwards. "Surely, Udora, you don't presume to believe them?"

"Now why wouldn't I believe them? Please, Charles. We mustn't offend the young ladies. They are much too well bred to dissemble. Pour a glass of sherry for each of them, if you please."

He reached for the decanter and poured a sippet of sherry into a glass for Em. She started to lift it to her lips when Udora stayed her arm.

"One moment, my dear. Charles, love. Don't be so stingy. Pour them each a full glass."

He apparently missed the significant look in her eyes, but he glowered and proceeded to fill the girls' glasses to the brim.

Taz looked as smug as Udora's cats when she gave them a dish of cream. The girl thanked Charles and batted her eyelashes in a poor imitation of a flirt before tossing off a goodly portion of the sherry in a single gulp. She began gasping before the wine was halfway down. What little remained in her glass spilled over the front of her ugly brown dress.

Udora patted the girl's back. "Oh, dear! I find that sipping my sherry is more conducive to enjoyment. Charles, be a pet and refill Taz's glass."

Charles scowled and started to protest, but Udora silenced him with a glance. Topaz jerked back quickly, holding the offending glass behind her back. "No." Her enormous blue eyes were glazed but she recovered quickly when she glanced sideways and saw the merriment writ on Udora's face. "No thank you, Mr. Willingsly." She lifted her chin defiantly. "One is quite enough. I—I had several glasses of sherry earlier in the day." She coughed again, then spoke in a strangled voice. "M-my father taught us that one m-must not overindulge."

A challenging glance at Udora met with an agreeable nod. "Excellent advice, Taz. Em, Amy? Would you like Charles to freshen your sherry?" It was obvious they had barely sipped the wine before setting the glasses down. "No?" Udora asked. "Well, in truth, I, too, am quite satisfied. Perhaps we'll save it for another time.

"However, the one good thing about sherry is that it does tend to take the chill off. Tell me, isn't there usually a fire in the grate?"

Amy shook her toast-brown curls. "We don't use the library much since... since Mama and Pappa..." Her voice drifted off.

"Yes, I see," Udora said. "Had I but known, I would have asked Mrs. Kragen to have the fire laid." Her eyes danced with mischief. "I wonder, Taz, perhaps you could perform a bit of your magic?" she said, waggling her fingers.

Charles looked confused. The girls gasped and Topaz's cheeks turned pink. She shrugged. "It's rather late for a fire, isn't it? I think d-dinner is about to be s-served."

SOMEHOW THEY MANAGED to survive the meal. Charles merely picked at his food, grumbling both about the service and the limited menu, which consisted of only a highly seasoned turtle soup, overcooked pheasant, three meat courses and a watery pudding. The bread was excellent. After his third piece, even Charles grudgingly admitted to its light texture and heavenly aroma.

Udora spent most of the meal observing the table manners, or lack of them, of the three girls. She wondered if they had never been taught proper etiquette, or if their manners, along with everything else, had simply fallen into neglect during the many months since their parents' death. She sighed, trying to imagine what it would be like for these child-women when in little more than a year they would be forced to enter the Marriage Mart. There wasn't a hope in heaven that any self-respecting mother would allow her son within a dozen yards of these ill-mannered, unrefined young ladies.

Em managed to consume more than the other diners put together, Amy ate very little and Taz ate nothing at all, despite Udora's encouragement. She did, however, under the influence of the sherry, contrive to keep everyone highly amused with her antics. Finally Udora gave up.

"Enough of this chirping merry, Taz. You must put something in your stomach besides the sherry else you will be painfully ill when morning comes."

Taz speared a gravy-soaked chunk of pork and waved it in the air. "Mama's gone. Pappa's gone and m-morning m-may nev-never come, so l-let's stand on the t-table and d-dance." She put her foot on her chair and started to get up, but she was too unsteady. The fork flew from her hand, landing in Charles's lap with a loud splat. Udora knew from the sick expression on his face that the pork had left a significant spot of grease on his immaculate inexpressibles.

He swore competently until a look from Udora silenced him. Had he not appeared so outraged Udora wouldn't have smiled, her amusement but slipped past her control.

He took one look at her face, jumped up from the table and slammed his fist down so hard that the goblets clinked together as if someone were playing the chimes.

Taz giggled. "I th-think I re-remember our music t-tutors s-strumming that song."

Charles bent to retrieve his chair, which had fallen over. At that moment the rear seam in his breeches gave way with a sickening sound leaving a narrow expanse of his unmentionables exposed to view. He straightened quickly, one hand covering his backside while his face flushed a deep scarlet.

"You did this, you heathens. You tampered with my seams," he said, shaking his finger at the three girls. "Udora, this is the outside of enough. Send Maggie up to pack. We're leaving this place in the morning."

"Girls, go upstairs at once," Udora's tone brooked no argument. Nevertheless, Taz looked as if she had every intention of remaining until Em and Amy took her hands to lead her from the room.

Udora tried to calm herself before confronting Charles, but this time she knew her feminine wiles would not serve her well enough to dissuade him from his chosen course. His ungentlemanly behaviour assured her of that fact. He was leaving. If she didn't want to lose him she would have little choice but to accompany him back to London.

"Charles, I'm so dreadfully sorry. I know this entire episode has been one disappointment after the other to you."

He gripped the back of the chair, striving to regain his temper. "To me? Does that mean that you are happy with the outcome of this supposed inheritance?"

"I would not pretend to be happy about it, my dear. Suffice it to say that I, too, am disappointed, if not discouraged."

He sighed in apparent relief, then came over to put his arm around her. "Dear lady. I should have known I could put my trust in you to see things as I see them. To stay longer would but serve to delay our marriage. And that, old girl, is something I could not bear." He kissed her fondly on the cheek and patted her shoulder. "We'll leave immediately after breakfast. If you wish, we can stop by at the solicitor's office in town and explain everything to Dorrance Watley."

She nodded as he continued. "As for now, I'll send round to the kitchen and order Maggie above stairs to pack your clothes."

Udora would have argued but no matter how one cut the cake, their departure was inevitable. She *was* getting old. When she saw Charles so disenchanted, she was reminded that as a woman just turned thirty, needless to mention four times widowed, her opportunities for wedded bliss were rapidly diminishing. If Charles left without her, he might choose to end their betrothal. She loved him too much to allow that to happen. Or, she amended, too honest to let the thought slip by her, if she weren't as enamoured of him as she had been of her other four husbands, she would soon *learn* to love him. He was dear to her in many ways.

No, she couldn't lose him. The thought hurt too much for her even to consider it, she decided as she climbed the staircase to her rooms.

The bedchamber seemed too quiet when Udora found herself standing beneath the darkened dome. No rustlings, no disembodied footsteps in the wall, no sense of any ghostly presence. Somehow their absence was disappointing. But she was unable to dwell on her curiously surprising thoughts, for Maggie bounced into the room, her shoe-button eyes sparkling with excitement.

"Is it true wot 'e says? We're goin' 'ome to The Lark's Nest?"

"Yes, I suppose it is. If we are to be ready to leave after breakfast we'll have to begin packing tonight."

"Yes, ma'am, whatever you say."

Udora shot Maggie a significant look. She couldn't remember the last time her abigail had been so respectful. Maggie dashed round to the adjoining room and returned with a pair of valises.

"I'll just pack the gowns and the things you won't be needin' and save what little else 'til tomorrow mornin'."

"You needn't be so happy about leaving," Udora said, feeling resentful about being forced into an awkward decision.

"Yes, ma'am. But iffen 'twas me who 'ad been stuck wi' the likes o' them three girls, I wou'n't be pullin' a long face if someone took me away from them. Even if 'twas Mr. Willingsly, stiff as 'e is," she said. Then she hurriedly added, "you weren't meant to rusticate. Not wi' your blunt and your good looks an foin figger. You ain't gettin' any younger. But then none o' us is."

"Thank you for reminding me."

"Yes, my lady."

They worked together in silence until most of the packing was finished. Then Udora washed her face in cold water and undressed for bed. It was just moments later when she heard Maggie snoring in the adjoining room.

As for herself, the night seemed to stretch interminably. She stared above her at the glass dome where the moon and drifting clouds caused amber light to flicker across the room. Withdrawing her hand from beneath the warm counterpane she let the moonlight ring her fingers like a wedding band of living gold. When she flexed her hand the light slid down to her wrist. *Shackles,* she mused, and then laughed at her own childish imagination. Whatever made her think of shackles? Charles? No. She knew enough about gentlemen to be able to manage him most of the time. But was that what she wanted? A man who would bend to her every wish? A man who could be manipulated? She closed her eyes tightly.

Her senses were suddenly assailed by the vision of a black-caped rider sitting astride a huge stallion high on a rocky escarpment. Then, without bidding, he approached and she could smell his scent, could know without touching, the strength of his hands, his shoulders . . . his loins. She groaned and turned on her side in an effort to banish the image from her mind.

It seemed like only minutes but it must have been hours later when she felt herself being pulled from the sweetness of a dream. He had come to her. She could feel his weight on the side of the bed, feel his hand touching her shoulder through the linen.

She reached out to draw him closer but the human contact brought her upright in bed.

"My lady, please wake up."

Udora groaned and fell back against the pillows. This was no phantom lover come to spirit her away in the night. "Wh-what is it? Who is there?" she demanded, seeing only a dark form leaning over her.

"It's me, Amy. We need you, my lady. Taz is sick. I think she's dying. You must come at once."

Udora was instantly awake. She pushed the girl aside and threw back the covers. "Where is she?"

"In our room."

"Show me."

They ran down the corridor together, and through the open doorway. A lighted candle faintly illuminated the two girls seated on the floor. Em had her arm round Taz who was doubled over in pain.

"Let me," Udora bent down. "Help me lift her onto the bed." Together they managed to accomplish the task. Udora tried to remember what one did for a sick child. She felt her forehead and asked Taz where the pain was worst. Taz could hardly speak but Em volunteered the information that Taz had been retching.

Udora nodded. "I thought as much. It's the wine. I doubt there is anything to worry about as long as we keep her quiet and comfortable."

Amy, looking tiny and angelic in her white cotton nightgown, was on the verge of tears. "But she hurts so much. There must be something we can do."

Udora sighed and sat down next to Taz on the bed. "A dish of hot tea would be the thing. I suppose we could wake Mrs. Kragen."

"No!" Taz cried out. "She mustn't know."

"Yes, I take your point," Udora agreed. She sat for a moment, stroking the girl's back. To Udora's surprise, Taz leaned closer. A moment later she was curled in the crook of Udora's arm. Udora could not identify the strange sensation that seemed to make her glow.

"I—I suppose we could heat some tea in my room," she said. "There are still hot coals in the fireplace and I carry a jar of tea for just such occasions. Taz, would you care to come into my bed for the rest of the night?"

Taz nodded, still unwilling to move from her warm nest. Udora reached round and pulled a quilt from the foot of the bed. "Here wrap this round you so you'll stay cosy." She helped her to a standing position, then faced the other girls. "Em, Amy? Will you be all right?"

They nodded.

"Very well. Back into bed then, before you take a chill." She saw the worried expression on their faces and her voice softened. "She's going to be fit as a fiddle in the morning. Well, save for an aching head," she said, with a twinkle in her eyes. "Wine can do that to you." She turned at the doorway. "Sleep well, girls."

Udora kept the blanket around Taz until she helped her into bed. Then she went about the business of making Taz a soothing cup of tea. It took a while to heat the dipper of water over the dying coals but when it was boiling Udora brewed a cup and stood over Taz while she drank it down. A half hour later Taz, sound asleep, had curled herself into a ball in the warm comfort of the bed. It had been a lesson hard learned, one she would remember.

But for Udora the hope of sleep had all but passed. What was it that Publius Syrus said about wine? "Wine has drowned more than the sea." Suffice to say tonight had been a shattering experience. Feelings she had never felt before were making themselves known. Strong feelings, yet somehow not unwelcome. The question was, could she control them?

She blinked back the tears which threatened to overwhelm her and refused to dwell on her drowning hopes for the future. For this one thing she knew. She could no more desert these children than she could leave her dear sweet cats to the mercy of a storm. She was here to stay. Charles would have to accept that. Perhaps he would even stay to assist her. But even as the thought occurred to her she knew that he would return alone to London when morning came.

CHAPTER FOUR

CHARLES WAS unusually bright and full of himself when Udora greeted him at breakfast the next morning. But his ebullience was short-lived. He looked first boyishly confused and then vexed.

"A morning dress, Udora? I thought you'd be attired in a travelling costume, knowing how eager I am to be on our way. I do hope your bags are packed and ready to be loaded on to the barouche."

"Before you say anything, Charles, there is something I must say to you."

"Nothing can be so important that it can't wait until you've had your chocolate." He lifted the pot and was about to pour until he noticed the cup she held was shaking. Frowning mightily, he stepped back. "Listen, old girl, I know that look on your face. I would advise you to think twice before making an irrevocable decision."

"I'm afraid it's too late, my dear."

He slammed the pot down, causing a reddish-brown stain to spread across the white tablecloth. "Indeed? Then may I assume that you have elected to accept the guardianship of the children?"

"I have no other choice. They need me, Charles. It's as simple as that. Truth be told, they need *us*, for it would be difficult indeed to rear three children without a stepfather to guide them."

He blustered and strode to the window, hands locked behind his back. At last he turned. "But I am *not* a father, Udora, nor have I the least desire to become one. At least not to three grown heathens who smell as if they've slept in a stable."

"You see . . . that is the very reason that they need us."

"What I *see* is that your mind is made up."

"I'm afraid it is."

"You would choose them over me?"

"I had hoped not to have to choose."

"Then you were far too optimistic. I must tell you, my lady, that I cannot and will not wait for you to come to your senses. It is now or never."

"I thought that might be your answer." She slipped the engagement ring from her finger. "You'll be wishing to return this to your mother."

"Yes."

She expected him to struggle more but he snapped his heels and bowed. "So it's come to this, has it?"

"It is not my wish, I assure you, Charles, but I have no choice in the matter."

"If you'll excuse me then, I'll prepare to take my departure. I'm sure you will understand that I have no appetite for breakfast."

"What nonsense. You have a long journey ahead of you."

But he was not to be persuaded. He squared his shoulders, looked at her with a disappointed expression, then strode from the room.

Udora also was keenly disappointed, although she felt a sense of relief that their conversation had been reasonably civil. She knew, though, that the emptiness he left behind him would soon take root in her head.

Maggie didn't help one bit. Upon answering Udora's summons to the breakfast room and learning she had broken her engagement to Charles and would not be returning to London, she was so distraught that Udora gave her permission to return to London with Charles. In the end, however, Maggie could no more leave her mistress "in the hands o' these rustics," as she put it, than Udora could desert the girls.

Next, she summoned Mrs. Kragen who took the news with stoicism. "Dass zis mean you vill be staying on permanently, your ladyship?"

"Yes, Mrs. Kragen. Until the girls either wed or come into their majority...according to the terms of Lord Leighton's last will and testament."

"Humph. Ve vill see," she said as she returned the chocolate pot to its candle warmer.

"You seem sceptical, Mrs. Kragen."

"*Ja.* Zere have been others, you know. A tutor, sree nannies, more domestics zan I can count on my fingers. Zey come, zey go. Ze *kinder* see to zat."

"But you remained. I admire such dedication."

"Humph. Vere vould I go? I haff lived here since I vas a girl."

They were interrupted when the three girls, deliberately uncombed, unwashed and wearing yesterday's wrinkled gowns, crowded into the breakfast room.

Taz stopped, hands on hips. "I thought you were gone."

"And good morning to you, too, Miss Topaz." She smiled at the three girls. "Do sit down. As you see, I have decided to remain here as your guardian."

"But you can't."

"And why not, Emerald? It was your father's wish."

"He didn't even know you."

"Alas, that is true, but there is no one else. It seems that we are stuck with one another and we must learn to make the best of it."

"We'll see," Taz said, repeating Mrs. Kragen's sentiments.

Before Udora could respond, the girls disappeared through the doorway and could be heard running down the corridor that led, Udora assumed, to a rear exit.

"Where are they going?" Udora asked Mrs. Kragen.

"Who knows? Maybe zey go to Partridge Run."

Udora's mood lifted. "Partridge Run? Is the family in residence? Do they have children?"

"No *kinder*. The master iz not married. The *kinder* like to see ze baby birds."

"Oh, dear," Udora said, horrified. "We can't have that. They are too old to run wild and unchaperoned. I must go after them at once. Will you have Blodgett harness the gig for me? And see to it that he gives me a horse that is properly shod."

Udora all but ran upstairs to change into a driving costume. Maggie, looking stricken and woebegone, sat on the edge of her cot. "Oh, my lady, wot 'ave I done, sendin' 'is lordship off without me?" She moaned. "'Ere I am stuck in the country like a turnip."

"What's done is done, Maggie. I don't have time for your sullens right now. We must go to Partridge Run and retrieve the children."

Maggie's face brightened. "Partridge Run? Ain't that where that 'andsome Mr. Bently lives?"

Before Udora could fully answer, Maggie ran to the armoire and began flinging clothes onto the bed. "The black velvet boots or the sky blue, ma'am?"

"The blue, I think. They are more cheerful, and heaven knows, I could use some good cheer this morning."

IT OCCURRED TO UDORA that driving from Amberleigh to Partridge Run was like going from London's East End slums to the manicured confines of exclusive Mayfair.

Maggie leaned forward. "Look at that, m'lady. Peacocks! And the flower beds. Ain't they somethin', like?" She clasped her hands to her breast. "And look. You can see the 'ouse through the trees. Ain't it grand, though."

Udora was more impressed than she cared to admit. The Tudor manor-house was equal to many of the magnificent country homes she had been privileged to visit. But she wasn't there to sight-see. "I suppose that we should offer our card before descending upon the house, but I doubt that the master is in residence. First we must find the aviary. Mrs. Kragen said that the girls come to visit the baby birds."

She flicked the reins and the bay mare followed the road round to the rear of the house towards the stables. Maggie pointed at a building partially concealed behind a row of trees. "There it is, m'lady. I can tell by the screening."

Udora nodded and reined the horse into a clearing close to the entrance.

"Stay with the horse, Maggie, or find someplace to tie her."

"There's a ring on the post. You'd best not go in alone."

Udora flashed Maggie a speaking look and smiled. "If it's Mr. Bently you're hoping to see, my girl, I wouldn't get your hopes up. He strikes me as the kind of man who wouldn't suffer fools gladly."

Maggie grinned. "Yes m'lady, he is a right un, and all o' that. 'Ceptin' for 'is game leg, 'e could lift the skirt o' the duchess 'erself."

Udora shook her head in resignation as she opened the door to the aviary. She had to give Maggie credit, for Udora agreed Bently was indeed a "right un"!

A narrow whitewashed corridor opened onto a main room lined to the ceiling with screened brooding boxes of various sizes. It was a light, airy and surprisingly clean room. The clucking and chirping gave evidence that several different kinds of birds were raised here. Udora found the musky odour to be only slightly unpleasant. She crossed the straw-covered floor towards another room from where voices emanated.

Inside, the twins were seated on bales of straw while they talked to Aaron Bently who leaned against a post, whittling a piece of wood. Topaz sat on the floor, her skirts hitched up to her knees, her lap all but covered with downy chicks.

Bently was the first to become aware of her presence. He rose somewhat stiffly but bowed with a practised smoothness that belied his humble background. Udora noticed at once that he was impeccably dressed right down to the champagne shine on his Hessians. There was a hungry look about him which drew her immediate attention, but she made an effort to concentrate on what he was saying.

"Your ladyship, what, may I ask, brings us the honour of your visit?"

Udora's face froze. "Surely you needn't ask. Even a man in your position must realize that it is most unseemly for young ladies to visit a neighbour's stables without benefit of a chaperon. I've no doubt that your master would deem it unsavoury, or at the very least, inappropriate."

The girls looked quickly from Bently to Udora and then back again. In that brief moment she saw a signal pass from Bently to the girls, but she was too distraught to venture a guess as to its meaning.

"I am certain, Mr. Bently, that the girls have told you of my decision to remain on at Amberleigh, according to the terms of their father's will."

He bowed his acknowledgement as she continued. "Very well, with that thought in mind, I would like to speak to you alone, providing your master would have no objection. As to you girls, go home at once. I will attend to you after you've seen to your morning ablutions."

For some reason it seemed they could barely restrain their laughter, a fact which considerably annoyed as well as surprised Udora, but a slight nod from Bently sent them on their way without further ado.

Udora frowned. "Should we not consult with the master of the house before I, uh..." She glanced at the partly finished carving. "Before I take you away from your work?" she asked drily.

He motioned towards a doorway that appeared to lead into an office. "I believe you will be more comfortable in here, Lady Udora. As to the other, I am very much my own master here at Partridge Run."

Udora felt ill at ease that this man in his menial position should be so comfortably assured of himself. Obviously, it concerned him not at all that he had been caught in unsavoury circumstances, nor that he had been chastised for his lack of adherence to proper social behaviour. Although his position demanded a certain amount of respect, Bently was still a mere bailiff.

Granted, the man was well groomed. It occurred to her as she passed close to him when he opened the door that he smelled temptingly masterful with a hint of bayberry which was used in a popular but costly shaving paste. She frowned thoughtfully. He wouldn't be the first menial to sample his master's toiletries. Nevertheless, she found the scent appealing. But for a well-trimmed moustache he was clean-shaven with now neatly shorn dark locks, which curled slightly behind his ears.

When he bent forward to seat her, she glanced up at him and suddenly the air seemed too heavy to breathe.

His moustache pulled up at the corners as if he regarded her with amusement. "You seem a bit distraught, Lady Udora. Are you quite comfortable?"

"Quite," she said shortly. Udora was grateful for the moment or two he required to go around the end of a makeshift table and seat himself. She took herself firmly in hand.

"Now then, Mr. Bently, I will endeavour to make this brief. First of all, I must ask that you cease and desist allowing the girls to visit you in the stables unescorted. While I would not dream of accusing you of unseemly behaviour, it is appearances which concern me. I am sure you understand."

He nodded. "Indeed. Until now, the girls have been almost completely without supervision. May I say how pleased I am that you and your fiancé have decided to take up residence at Amberleigh?" He paused overlong.

Udora had not expected him to be so understanding. Nor had she intended to discuss her broken engagement, but before she could stop herself, she had told him everything. His gaze never left her face.

"May I offer my congratulations," he said, a smile lighting his eyes.

"I beg your pardon!" Udora said coldly. "Surely you are not so uncouth as to believe that congratulations are in order at a time such as this?"

His eyes grew dark with an intensity which shook her to the soles of her feet. "Forgive me, my lady, if I offend you. You have informed me that you are twice widowed, but in truth, you are far too innocent where men are concerned. Charles Willingsly is hardly the man for you."

She jumped to her feet and he rose immediatley. "Of all the unmitigated gall! You forget yourself, sir. Must I remind you of your position?" She found herself sputtering, and she clenched her hands at her side. "I'll have you know that Charles Willingsly is one of the most eligible bachelors in London. He is a perfect match for me. And who are you to offer an opinion?" She sat down again and he followed suit.

He shrugged. "At present, I am only an interested neighbour. But it appears I have misjudged you, my lady. I had no idea that your taste in husbands might run towards the lap-dog variety."

"What utter nonsense. I..." In her agitation she all but leaped out of her chair again.

"Do sit down, Lady Udora. All this jumping up and down is tiresome." He stretched out his lame leg into a more comfortable position. "Perhaps we should change the topic. Was there something else you wished to chastise me for?"

She saw the glint of humour in his eyes, and though she willed it otherwise, her temper began to cool. Devil take the man! He was charming when he tried to be but she was not about to let him know it.

"Very well, we shall speak on other subjects; however, in future I'll thank you to confine your remarks to other than my personal affairs...matters," she amended, then could have kicked herself for doing so. The glint in his eyes attested to the fact that he had not missed her unfortunate choice of words.

She adjusted her driving skirt. "Were it not for the fact that you were so helpful to me yesterday, I would not be calling upon you, but I perceive I require your advice."

"You have no need to apologize, my lady."

She saw that he was laughing at her, though no sound came from his lips. The laughter was in his eyes, those devilishly compelling dark eyes that never seemed to leave hers. Her voice sent a chill through the small room. "Do not misunderstand, Mr. Bently. It was not meant as an apology. Only an explanation."

"I stand corrected. Do go on. How may I be of service?"

"As you so accurately pointed out, something must be done about Dodson. The man must be turned off, but the question is, how do I find someone to replace him? Considering how much the estate has deteriorated, I feel that we need someone with outstanding qualifications who can manage farmlands the size of Amberleigh."

He leaned his elbows on the table and rested his chin on his hands. "I fear that will be a problem not easily solved. Of course we can enquire round the neighbouring towns and villages, but I doubt that you will find a qualified man who is not already employed. At the very least the search could take a year or more."

Udora was aghast. "A year or more? But that is impossible. We need a bailiff at once."

He shook his head and sighed. "A pity."

"No. I refuse to accept defeat before I've even begun." She scooted her chair up to the table and leaned close to him. "Tell me, Mr. Bently. Would you be available for hire, assuming the substantial salary met with your satisfaction?"

Bently looked shocked. "My lady! Surely you aren't suggesting that I forgo my loyalty to the master of Partridge Run? Under the circumstances I consider it immoral or at the very least underhanded for you to even suggest such a thing."

Udora felt her face turn red. "I didn't mean it to appear so. If the master were present I would most assuredly speak with him. Forgive me if I have spoken out of turn." Noting his smug expression, she cursed herself for apologizing.

"You must understand," she said, "that I would do anything to help those dear girls regain their place in Society."

Bently was beginning to enjoy this little game. Udora Middlesworth obviously knew her way around the drawing-rooms of Mayfair but she was out of her depth in Coventry. Seeing the pious expression on her face, he tilted his head back in a hearty laugh. "Dear girls, my eyes! The three of them are hell-cats and we both know it." He enjoyed shocking her, but enjoyed her heated response even more.

"Guard your tongue, sir. Remember your position. The girls may not be titled but they are Quality and they deserve to be treated with respect."

He laughed, then regarded her steadily. "If I may be so bold, my lady. Pray do not play the noble benefactor with me. Your opinion of those *dear girls* is writ all over your face. You'd like nothing better than to shake the impudence out of them and scrub them with lye soap from top to bottom."

Udora started to protest but was disconcerted by the knowledge that he would know the untruth of it. The thought was not reassuring. Contriving to look disdainful, she rose to go. "I believe I have taken more than enough of your valuable time, Mr. Bently. If you will excuse me."

He rose at the same moment and came round the end of the table to place his hand on her arm. "There will be conditions, you know."

"Conditions? I—I don't understand." What she did understand was that his hand was on her arm shooting bolts of lightning through her veins.

"Conditions of my employment."

"You mean that you might be willing..." She caught herself just in time, before she had a chance to plead. Drawing herself up to her full height—which unfortunately brought the top of her head to only just beneath his chin—she managed a modicum of dignity. "Am I to understand that you are interested in hiring on as bailiff of Amberleigh?"

He loomed over her, brown eyes meeting blue in silent challenge. "I am more than interested."

The scoundrel. He knew that she was awake enough to recognize the double meaning of his words. Udora darted a quick tongue across her lips, then sucked in her breath. "Be good enough to unhand me, sir."

"My apologies. I only meant to steady you. You seemed a trifle unsure on your feet."

"Indeed!" It was obvious that neither of them believed for one moment that she had suddenly become feeble. And yet when he withdrew his hand Udora noticed that she was trembling.

She took three steps backwards. Her voice had become husky and she cleared her throat. "You...you mentioned conditions. Just what are they? As to your stipend, I know we can come to an agreement. In addition you...and your family," she said, lowering her eyelashes in embarrassment, "could, uh, take over the bailiff's house for your residence."

Bently was amused. "If you are referring to a wife and children, I am quite alone. And as you well know, the bailiff's house is a pigsty. It would be best burned to the ground."

A female flutter began somewhere in the region of her breastbone. Drat him that he could so easily cause such feelings with a mere lift of an eyebrow or quirk of his moustache.

He continued. "No, my lady. The conditions I have differ considerably from what you propose." He sat on the edge of the table and stretched his lame leg out in front of him.

"Partridge Run operates smoothly enough now that I need only supervise the men who do the actual work. I do not propose to give that up. I will, however have the freedom to devote most of my time to taking over the management of Amberleigh." He paused as if to emphasize a point. "Provided, that is, that I am given a free hand to run it as I see fit."

"I presume you don't mean to do so without supervision." The silence seemed interminable. Finally he crossed his arms in front of him and fixed her with his glare. "And who would you suggest to oversee my work? The barrister, Mr. Watley?"

"Hardly, considering the sorry condition he permitted the estate to fall into." She lifted her chin in a defiant gesture. "You would, of course, report to me."

"Ah! Then you would make the decisions when and in what fields to plant the crops and what stock to buy." He seemed to warm to the subject. "And which ewes to breed to which ram."

"Enough!" She raised her hands to hide her flaming face. "You've made your point, Mr. Bently. Until such time as I am more knowledgeable about the workings of the estate, I will leave the decisions to you."

He nodded in satisfaction. "There is one more thing."

"Dare I ask?" she queried drily.

His well-trimmed moustache lifted as he smiled. "I suspect there is not much you *wouldn't* dare, my lady. But to answer your question, I will need an office in the main house."

She looked up quickly. "Why the main house? There are several buildings that you should find suitable as a place to work."

"That would be true, were I to take up residence at the estate, but inasmuch as I plan to remain living at Partridge Run, we will need a place where the records can be safely kept and yet always available to me...or to you. I think you'll find it much less awkward to, ah, supervise me if we are under the same roof."

Udora stared at him, waiting for the telltale twinkle in his eyes that betrayed his teasing, but he was remarkably controlled. She was alarmed by her inability to assess this man. If there was one area in which she might be considered an expert, it was men. Instinct had rarely let her down. She knew the precise moment her men had set their caps for her. She knew when they were lying. She knew when they were tempted to stray, though truth be told, none of her husbands had lived long enough to tire of her. But this man was different. She sensed that he could give her a run for her money, should she be unwise enough to let him get the upper hand. *Pistachions!* she thought. *I'm beginning to act as henwitted as Maggie on her worst days.*

She sighed. "Very well, Mr. Bently. I will see to it that a room is made ready for you. When do you wish to begin?"

"Tomorrow."

"So soon? Will you be able to obtain permission from your employer that quickly to take on another position?"

"Leave all to me, my lady. I assure you the master of Partridge Run is most generous."

"Then I am forever indebted to him."

His eyes glittered. "Indeed. I know he will be more than pleased to hear that. I will be at Amberleigh tomorrow morning at ten."

"So early?"

"No. So late. I thought to allow you time to get the room in readiness. In the future I will arrive at eight." He bowed and gestured towards the door.

Udora knew she was being dismissed, but to give him the advantage was worse than unthinkable. She stiffened. "Sit down, Mr. Bently. I think we need to discuss your stipend before I take my leave."

He shrugged. "Your wish is my command, my lady."

"And that is the way it should be, is it not?" She smiled to dilute the sting of her words.

Bently eased himself back into the chair without once removing his gaze from Udora's face. *Fascinating!* he thought. Quentin Thackery had talked at length about Lady Udora just after her marriage to Harvey Thackery a few years ago. Even though Quentin had never met Udora he had admired her and followed her colourful trail after her husband's death. Quentin, always the faithful husband, nevertheless had an eye for an intelligent woman and the fact that she was also beautiful and spirited only added to her appeal. Bently cursed himself for carrying on where Quentin had left off. She intrigued him as no other woman had. A Society woman, God's teeth! And now she was no longer the fantasy woman he could only imagine at night before he went to sleep. She was here, in this very room. And she was going to pose a problem.

CHAPTER FIVE

A HALF-HOUR LATER Udora picked up her reticule and prepared to depart. "I think, Mr. Bently, that our arrangement will work to both our advantage. If you can do for Amberleigh what you've done for Partridge Run, I'll consider it nothing short of a miracle."

"I'll do my best, your ladyship." He bowed and brushed his lips against her hand before helping her into the gig.

Although Udora had never been impressed by the customary token kiss on the hand, this time it was different. She didn't expect the courtesy from a menial. Moreover, it would have been impossible to anticipate the surge of heat which suffused her whenever they chanced to touch. If anything, it became more pronounced with each encounter.

That she could experience such feelings now of all times struck her as odd. Her betrothal to Charles had been dead scarcely long enough for *rigor mortis* to set in. Maybe Bently had been in the right of it when he congratulated her on her broken engagement for, in point of fact, he hadn't been the first to tell her that Charles wasn't man enough for a woman such as herself. Still, she missed him now that he had removed to London. There was no doubt in her mind that had she gone ahead with her plan to wed, Charles could have been moulded into quite an acceptable husband.

Maggie sounded petulant as Udora placed the rug over her lap. "It's done, then? We're stayin' on 'ere?"

"Yes, I thought I had made that clear."

Bently handed Udora the reins. "What is it, Maggie?" he asked, regarding her with interest. "Are you already missing the Town? Or is it some young man you've left behind?"

"None what I would settle for," Maggie said, fluffing her hair. "O' course they stand a few steps 'igher than most o' the rustics I've seen 'ereabouts, present company excepted."

He smiled. "Then we'll have to do something about that, won't we?"

Maggie apparently chose to assume that he was offering his own services because she opened up like a flower turning its face to the sun. "Fancy that," she said, smiling widely. "I'm beginnin' to see as how I could learn to like this foin country air."

Udora had seen enough. She snapped the reins over the mare's back and turned her towards the lane. "We'll be expecting you tomorrow, Mr. Bently," she said, calling back over her shoulder. "Good day."

He clicked his heels and bowed.

Udora turned to Maggie with a scathing look. "Fresh air, my eyes! It's Mr. Bently's scent that tickles your nose, not the smell of sweetgrass growing in the meadow. And whatever happened to the weeds and dung piles you waxed so eloquently about on the drive over here?"

"That was Amberleigh. This is Partridge Run," Maggie said, looking more henwitted than usual.

But Udora found it impossible to chastise the girl when she herself was hard-pressed to keep an innocent thought in her head. *Dear Heaven,* she mused. How on earth will we manage to preserve our decorum with that man all but living in the same house?

TIME AND the press of duties proved to be the answer. When Udora and Maggie arrived back at Amberleigh that day, it was to find their clothing once again packed and their valises waiting at the front door. Udora, admiring the girls their pluck but refusing to let it show, promptly ordered the luggage to her sitting-room, then sent word with Dulcie for the girls to meet her there. In the meantime Udora spoke with Mrs. Kragen and ordered refreshments to be sent upstairs.

Probably more out of curiosity than a wish to be obedient, the girls assembled as they were bade to do. Their eyes alight with mischief, they stood waiting for the expected reprimand, but Udora greeted them with a congenial smile. "Now, then, you've been the busy ones, haven't you? Do sit down. I thought we might have a glass of lemonade and a biscuit or two while I show you a few secrets. Mrs. Kragen makes wonderful apricot crisps, doesn't she?"

Udora took the oil lamp from the table and set it on the floor. "Maggie, be good enough to put my valise on one end of the table and open it for us."

The girls looked surprised, confused and apprehensive. Udora sipped her lemonade, then set the glass on the floor as well. She lifted a wrinkled gown from the valise and held it up.

"While I appreciate the fact that you're trying to become accomplished at womanly tasks, I think you'll find it much easier if you first have some instructions. And that's why I'm here, isn't it? I recall the first time I was sent off to board-school. It took weeks for me to remove all the wrinkles from my dresses. Madame took away my privileges for five whole days."

The girls giggled. Udora smiled. "Of course we sometimes do things the hard way, but it saves so much time if we learn to do them correctly. For example, packing a valise. Your maid will eventually take over that duty, but chances are that you will first have to instruct her."

She shot a look at her disgruntled abigail. "My Maggie is a genius at taking care of me. I wouldn't dream of going anywhere without her."

Maggie brightened and straightened her shoulders. Udora patted her arm. "I wonder, Maggie, if you could show the girls how these gowns should be folded so that they won't wrinkle when they're packed?"

While Maggie went about demonstrating the procedure of caring for m'lady's wardrobe, Udora hovered over her.

"Oh, girls, notice this blue taffeta. I first wore it to the Gallsworthy ball in Mayfair and you'll never credit what happened." She lowered her voice. "Well, I'll tell you but you mustn't whisper a word of it to anyone else. You see, Lord Beaverton was there with his wife who was broad as a barge across the beam. Well, lo and behold, this night she was well into her cups when she backed into a flambeau, knocked it over and burned the backside of her ball gown. Unfortunately, that night Lady Beaverton had chosen to go *au naturel*... where unmentionables were concerned."

Udora saw that she had caught their immediate attention. "And this one," she said, holding up a cashmere shawl, "caused me no small measure of embarrassment, though in the end, it stood me in good stead. My first husband, Thurgood, was determined to make a good impression on the Chancellor of the Exchequer for some political strategy he had in mind. We were guests at the minister's house, you see, and the good man was overly proud of a litter of puppies. He had handed one of them to me when all of a sudden, I felt an inexplicable warmth trickle down my leg. The shawl was sodden but worse still, the front of my gown had turned from pale blue to a frightful green. Well, the minister was embarrassed and there was little choice but to invite us to remain as house guests until the damage to the gown could be repaired. He located an identical shawl and sent it to me, but best of all, my husband and the minister became close friends and confidants."

Amy fingered an ivory velvet creation embroidered with seed pearls. "Tell us about this gown."

"That one I wore when Beau Brummel..." She chuckled, then placed the ivory velvet gown carefully in the armoire. "Ah, but I mustn't bore you with such flapdoodle."

Emerald clasped her hands together. "Oh, do tell us more." Udora gave her a quick hug. "Another time, sweetling. Now when you're a little more experienced, I will let each one of you try folding a gown."

Emerald ran her hand across a filmy negligee. "It doesn't look so hard. I could do it right now."

"Oh, I hardly think so," Udora said, feigning grave doubts. Finally she spread her hands. "Very well, I suppose you may try."

Emerald stood and leaned forward, taking great care to fold the garment exactly as she had been instructed. Udora clasped her hands together. "There now. Aren't you full of surprises? I had no idea you were so capable."

Emerald smiled, pushing her spectacles back up her nose. "It really was not so very difficult."

Amy jumped up. "May I try, too?"

Though she was less adroit, Amy managed quite well and Udora praised her. Looking over at Taz, who leaned against the wall, Udora smiled. "Taz, I suppose you would also like to take a turn?"

"I ain't no servant." Without another word she left the room. Emerald and Amy, looking a trifle apologetic, followed after her.

Shortly after the girls had left Udora and Maggie began to hear the odd rustlings in the wall next to the fireplace once again. Maggie was so overset that Udora was forced to send her downstairs to assist in preparing Bently's office next to the library.

Udora had chosen that particular room with its tapestries and fine woodwork, even though it was far too grand to be used as a workroom. Maggie, being the sly-boots that she was, didn't hesitate to make a great to-do over the connecting door to the library. . . the room in which Udora would be spending most of her waking hours.

Udora felt compelled to defend her choice. "Of course I could have selected a room at the other end of the corridor, but it doesn't make sense, does it? Mr. Bently will have questions which need to be discussed and it will save time if he doesn't have to come looking for me."

"Or you to go lookin' for 'im," Maggie said. She slanted a quick glance at Udora who was arranging writing materials in a desk drawer. The remark was so innocently spoken that Udora wasn't certain how to interpret it. But before Udora could query her on her meaning, Maggie had the good sense to turn her back and suddenly become very industrious.

Udora bit back a reprimand. Maggie was, after all, her only ally in this house of tribulation. And she did keep Udora amused.

The news that Aaron Bently would be established in an office next to the library caused no little stir in the household. Most of the staff expressed pleasure, with the exception of Mrs. Kragen.

"Vell, don't expect me to clean and dust in zere. I haff enough to do vitout zat."

Udora nodded. "I certainly agree. You'll be pleased to know that I've sent to London for some of my own household staff, and they should be arriving early next week."

Mrs. Kragen blanched. "Does this mean I vill be turned off?"

"That depends on you, Mrs. Kragen. Would you like to continue on as housekeeper? Mrs. McMasters is my housekeeper, but I am certain there is enough work to keep you both quite busy. And Mr. Mc-

Masters is my butler. I think you will find him most congenial, although he is a bit of a high-stickler.

Udora paused. "There would of course be some changes. I could not permit things to continue as they are now."

Mrs. Kragen stiffened. "If you don't like the vay I do things . . ."

"I meant no such thing," Udora replied promptly. "No one could have done better under the circumstances, but you must realize that circumstances have changed and you must also change if you wish to remain in my employ." She observed that the woman was weakening. "Why not wait until my servants arrive before making a decision. I'm sure you will get on quite well with them."

Mrs. Kragen sniffed, but reserved any comment she might have made as she went back to work. The sour expression on her face was mute testimony to her displeasure.

THE ORMULU CLOCK in the library was striking ten when Bently arrived the following morning... *through the front door!* Udora could scarcely conceal her annoyance. Mrs. Kragen, acting surprisingly congenial, ushered him in to the library with more respect than she had accorded anyone, save the solicitor, Mr. Watley.

She actually smiled and inclined her head towards Udora. "Do you vish refreshment, my lady?"

Udora was too surprised by her sudden cooperation to respond immediately. Bently assumed control.

"Nothing for me, Mrs. Kragen. Perhaps her ladyship would care for something?"

Udora recovered immediately. "Not now, Mrs. Kragen. Thank you. You may go." She turned to Bently. "If you will follow me, I'll show you to your office." Without waiting for his response, she sailed past the book-lined walls, through the connecting doorway, and into the newly furnished room.

Initially she intended to decorate the room in elegant harmony, but the more Udora thought on it, the more she felt it necessary to impress upon Mr. Bently that it was *she* who was in charge. At the last moment she had requested the removal of the beautifully carved desk and bookcases she had ordered brought from another room. She then had them replaced with a set of worn chairs, table, and several shelves which would have looked more at home in Bently's aviary.

Bently's reaction was disappointing. He ran his hand across the makeshift table. "Marvellous grain. Sturdy, too. You don't often find such lovely, simple furniture as this these days."

Udora felt his gaze upon her and she blushed like a debutante in her first Season. "I have a more comfortable chair which would fit nicely in the window alcove. I'll request that someone bring it down this afternoon," she said, only to regret seconds later that she had weakened so soon.

"Whatever you wish, my lady, though you must not go to trouble on my account. The arrangements are quite satisfactory. Now if you will permit a suggestion, someone must see to Dodson. I would like to begin at once to perform my duties as bailiff. Of course Dorrance Watley must be informed of your decision and I should be happy to deliver him your notice of authorization."

Udora admired his efficiency but at the same time felt that he was underestimating her capabilities. She straightened. "I have just this morning sent a notice round to the solicitor's office informing him that I have agreed to the terms of Quentin Thackery's will. I have also advised him that you will replace Dodson and I mean for both of us to call on the bailiff as soon as we have completed our business here."

She pointed to a stack of ledgers lying on the table. "You'll find most of the records there. I have not yet discovered where the current books are kept, but I will give them to you when I've had a chance to locate them."

"Dodson most likely has them. Are you certain you wish to be present? The man is unpleasant enough even when he has not been imbibing."

Udora drew her shawl around her. "Thank you, but I choose to accompany you. I'll order my gig sent round."

"No need to bother. My gig is waiting in front."

Udora looked up at him and their gaze locked for an excruciating moment. It was with considerable effort that Udora turned away in order to recover her composure. Having done so, she returned to face him coolly. "Mr. Bently, you have a way of anticipating my every move. I'm not entirely certain I like that feature in my servants."

He was predictably unscathed by her deliberate slight. "Do not be confused, Lady Udora. It is the *farm* I serve. At least until I have mastered it. Other concerns about similar features must be taken up later."

He had reached up to assist her to adjust her shawl, but as he did so, his fingers glided up her arm in an innocent yet somehow intimate touch. She shot him a suspicious look.

Was it deliberate? Udora wondered. If she mentioned he had overstepped himself, he might only laugh at her imaginings. And although he had left words unspoken, Udora knew he had told her in no uncertain terms that he was not *her* servant. Had she not been so dependent on him, it would have given her great pleasure to discharge him on the spot. But she knew she was not being honest with herself. *The devil take the man!*

However, it *was* with substantial relish that she turned off Dodson. Particularly after he boldly threatened serious harm to her person and to her family, present and past. One could plainly see that he was already on his way to a drunken stupor when they arrived. Udora was grateful to learn that he was not married, for to strip a man of gainful employment would have been made more difficult if he had had a family depending upon him for their financial support. As it was, she promised to make arrangements for his room and board at the local inn for a period of two months.

Bently had suggested she make the offer. She would have given Dodson a bag of coins in severance but Bently reminded her that the money would be gone before the cockcrow, and very likely Dodson would be back for more.

As the days passed Udora was too busy to think of anything but the work to be done. The McMasters were established in a well-appointed suite of three rooms. Having noticed that Mrs. Kragen was none too happy with the fuss Udora had been making over her own servants, Udora sent a comfortable chaise longue up to the woman's third-floor bedchamber.

Bently, who seemed to be on familiar terms with everyone in the village, suggested that Udora hire a farm couple and their three sons for additional help. They were good workers, and their cheerful presence brightened everyone's mood, save for that of Miss Topaz who, when not contriving some new mischief, remained in a state of the dismals.

Without doubt it was Taz who convinced the twins to revert to their sullen or at least indifferent behaviour. They kept to their rooms or stole quietly out of doors. Udora was fast losing patience. She had decided to swallow her pride and consult Bently, for it was to him whom the children most often turned with their questions. He would never let her forget that *she* had come to *him*, but it would be worth the price to bring a measure of peace to the family.

Family. How strange the word tasted on her lips. Even as a child growing up she had never had a sense of family. Truth be told, save for her four cats and the husband who had been the current resident, she had never felt the need to lean on anyone for support. Now she was the titular head of a family... and she wasn't sure that she was equal to the responsibility.

From the first day Mrs. Kragen had treated Aaron Bently like visiting royalty. Without consulting Udora she laid a cover for him at the dining table. Udora had been struck speechless as he had seated her and then taken the chair across from her. It was as if he thought it the most natural thing in the world. A few days later when one of the new servants was to supervise the dining room, the routine had already been so established that it would have been ludicrous to attempt to change it.

And it was pleasant, too much so for her own peace of mind, Udora thought, to have an intelligent and congenial man with whom to share her meals. Heaven knew that the three girls offered little in the way of companionship. It was only after she ordered Cook not to permit them food between meals that the girls managed to appear at table at the dinner hour.

One bright morning Udora wandered through the connecting doorway into Bently's workroom. He finished adding a column of numbers, then laid aside his pencil and looked up. "You look tired this morning, my lady. You've been working far too hard."

"It isn't the work I mind."

"I've noticed that. I find it strange that you were so much at home among London's upper ten thousand and yet you've managed to adapt so well to Amberleigh."

Udora settled into a Chippendale chair and rested her hands on the carved arms. "My father, the Marquess of Riddinghouse, believed that women are one of England's most underdeveloped resources. He insisted that I be educated beyond French, drawing and needlework offered to most young ladies. I soon found that I had an insatiable appetite for wide variety of learning."

"Aha. A bluestocking, are you? I never would have guessed. I picture you in a ball gown, your hair studded with diamonds and a dozen or so swains dancing attendance upon you."

Udora dimpled. "Suffice to say, I hid my love for books quite well, as any sensible woman would do. And I've had my share of attention since I was launched into Society." She shook her head in wonder. "But in all those years it never once occurred to me that I might sometime become responsible for shaping another person's future." She shook her head. "Of course there was Yvette Cordé. But Yvette was already a grown woman with a woman's intuitive grace and femininity." She laughed softly. "And now I've been given the Thackery Jewels."

His eyes sparkled. "Indeed. Topaz, Emerald and Amethyst. Though none of them quite resemble precious stones, don't you agree?"

His candour surprised her but she welcomed it. "Sometimes I wonder if I would be doing them a disservice to insist on come-outs for them and all which that entails."

"It's what their father wanted. Both Quentin and Marion expected them to take their rightful place in Society and to marry well."

Udora stiffened at his familiarity. "Quentin and Marion? Were they intimates of yours?"

He nodded, unperturbed. "Indeed. We had been on a first-name basis for years." He fixed her with a challenging gaze, knowing full well that he had her at a disadvantage. He rather liked the feeling. It wasn't easy to take the advantage from Udora Middlesworth, and he was going to savour it as long as he could.

"Forgive me," Udora said. "It will take time for me to become accustomed to country ways. After nearly a month I am not even used to the girls. I thought that allowing them to take off the black gloves would appease them, but they were not impressed. They were hardly even interested in their new wardrobe which the seamstresses are hurrying to complete." She pressed her fingertips together. "There must be some secret to making peace with children."

Bently felt a sudden rush of compassion. "Think back to your own childhood, my lady. Children are children. They have the same fears, the same uncertainties, the same hopes and dreams that we had as children."

"I can't imagine you having any fears."

His face creased into a broad smile. "There were one or two. Someday I'll tell you about them."

The anticipation pleased her. "Then tell me about your dreams."

"Now that, my lady, is truly a horse of a different colour." He stood up and walked round the end of the table. "I am off to visit a tenant farmer who is having a problem with moles in his vegetable garden. Would you care to join me?" He came over and reached for her hand, knowing that his cavalier use of intimate gestures never failed to provoke her, though it was curiously satisfying to sometimes unsettle her stuffy sensibilities. For a woman who was said to thrive on the outrageous, she could be remarkably stiff-rumped.

This time she barely hesitated, but accepted his hand and rose. "Yes, I believe I would like to accompany you. It's time I came to know our tenant families. Considering the way the farm has gone to seed, we may have to give thought to some changes."

"I wouldn't be too hasty, Lady Udora. I would first like a chance to work with them."

"Of course. The decision is yours."

It occurred to him that she was becoming too agreeable. Had she found him out? He studied her face. No, it was something else. She would have been livid had she discovered his little charade. At one time the prospect of witnessing Lady Udora fly into the boughs would have been utterly appealing, but as each day passed he became more uneasy about his deception.

Later, when he once more helped her into his gig, Udora marvelled at Bently's comfortable way with farm people. They welcomed him as an old friend and yet they seemed to respect him as if he were of the gentry.

The wives of the tenant farmers were at first shy with Udora, but, thanks to Bently, they warmed to her very quickly. Mrs. Kelsey, a babe under each arm and one at her skirts, tried to clear a place for Udora to sit. Bently, an innocent smile crinkling his eyes, promptly took one of the babies and handed it to Udora.

"There now, Mrs. Kelsey. That should give you another hand to work with. Her ladyship said just this morning that she wants very much to become acquainted with all the farm families."

Mrs. Kelsey stared at her in wonderment. "Be that the God's truth, your ladyship? Even the lady of the manor 'erself, God rest 'er soul, nivver took to call on us."

Udora smiled weakly as she attempted to adjust the wriggling child to a less awkward position. "Rest assured, Mrs. Kelsey, that I hope to make your lives more comfortable than they were before." The look she shot Bently could have singed his eyebrows had it been less chilly in the cottage. He quickly excused himself and went outside to speak to the woman's husband.

Fortunately, the baby smelled sweet and was not disposed to squall until a half hour later when Udora took her departure.

Mrs. Kelsey beamed. "There, and you see? Little Timmy has taken a likin' to you right off. You be that welcome anytime, m'lady."

Bently held the door for Udora, all the while grinning like a cat with a cornered mouse. Udora could almost feel the distance between them closing.

When Bently delivered her back to Amberleigh before continuing on his rounds, McMasters looking as polished and dignified as he had in Town, handed Udora a silver salver on which rested an invitation to tea from a nearby neighbour. Alicia Mellows, Lady Finecroft, who was currently in residence at Finecroft Hall, mentioned that her son, Phillip, and daughter, Constance, were on holiday from school. The invitation included the three Thackery girls. Udora secreted it into her tucker as she climbed the stairs.

At last her patience had begun to bear fruit. Granted, Alicia Mellows was of little significance to London Society, but it was an opportunity to introduce the girls to the social situations they would encounter during their first Season. No longer in deep mourning, they were free to entertain as well as be entertained. There was no better way to prepare them for the Marriage Mart.

She could scarcely contain her excitement as she went in search of them to share the news.

CHAPTER SIX

TEA AT FINECROFT HALL proved to be two steps short of a disaster. Lady Finecroft greeted them after the butler, who Udora guessed was a rustic recently elevated to the lofty post, ushered them to the salon. Udora immediately discounted Alicia Mellows as a fashion plate example of *á la modalité*. She was a full-figured woman whose tastes in colours ran to red, burgundy and a bilious green. Her son and daughter were her complete opposite. She introduced them with pride, contriving somehow to squeeze in the information that her son was a pupil of Sir Frederick Gault, and that her daughter was considered slap up to the mark in her French class at Miss Elizabeth Castor's School for Girls. To her credit, the lady managed not to blanch when Udora presented the Thackery girls dressed in their old and ill-fitted black bombazines.

Thanks to Taz, they had refused to wear their new gowns. Amy and Em looked adequately groomed, but Taz had not taken brush to hair since before Udora arrived at Amberleigh.

Phillip had the good taste to pay his respects to the visitors and then fade into the background. Constance was less inclined towards subtlety. Seating herself across from Topaz, she toyed with a silken black ringlet. "Is that really your own hair, Miss Topaz, or is it some kind of wig that you've worn as mourning attire?"

Taz, who was eying a bronze urn, looked ready to throw it. Udora laughed. "Oh, haven't you heard, Miss Constance? The tousled curl is the latest rage among the dandizette, for those who have the courage to wear it. In truth, Taz has complained that it is far too much bother to maintain, but agreed to keep it for one more day."

"You must show me how it is done, Miss Topaz," Constance begged. "I try so hard to stay *au courant*, but our head mistress is dreadfully behindhand."

Taz inclined her head in a regal gesture. "Yes, Miss Constance. One can see that. How awful for you."

For one brief moment Em stopped pushing her spectacles back up her nose and Amy stopped chewing her fingernails.

Phillip, sitting off to the side, surveyed them all with an expression of condescending disbelief. When his mother opened her tabatière and offered it to Udora, who declined the snuff with acceptable politeness, he quietly excused himself from the room.

Udora observed that his absence had not gone unnoticed by the three girls. She smiled to herself. Perhaps they were not as unpromising as she had thought. With introductions to the appropriate young men, the Thackery Jewels just might begin to sparkle. But before that they were in for a few surprises. And today was going to be the day, she vowed silently, all the while endeavouring to answer Lady Finecroft's barbed enquiries with a smile.

When they returned to Amberleigh, Aaron Bently was once again at his worktable in his office next to the library. He rose as Udora entered, but she motioned for him to stay seated. He observed that she carried a roll of pressed paper, which she spread out on one end of the table.

"I wonder Mr. Bently, if you could assist me?" She came around to his side of the table and stood next to him. He inhaled her fresh scent, which seemed to be emanating from the moss-green-and-yellow sprigged muslin she wore so fetchingly.

Her tone of voice always intrigued him. Sometimes so soft and appealing. Other times so cool and controlled. But never indifferent, he thought. By all that was holy, she was never indifferent.

"Mrs. Kragen has managed to unearth the original building plans of Amberleigh, Mr. Bently, and I wonder if you could explain what these markings here indicate?"

He leaned closer, allowing himself the luxury of brushing her shoulder. Despite himself his voice was husky when he spoke. "The room is above stairs. Your bedchamber, I presume?"

"That is correct. It is this area here by the fireplace which interests me."

"Yes. I see what you mean. There appears to be a very narrow passageway, no more than three feet, according to the scale, and it begins here in this linen closet in the hallway and ends in a stairway leading down to the main floor."

"Aha. Just as I thought."

"I beg your pardon?"

"That will explain the rustlings in the wall. I suspect the girls have been up to their usual tricks."

He grinned. "So you caught them out? I wagered you would be too discerning to allow them to best you. Has Taz demonstrated her ability to start a fire with magic?"

"Ah, yes indeed. An old trick with a wick, a live coal and a small measure of whale oil. I learned that one back in board-school."

He chuckled. "I rest assured you have *many* hidden talents." He tapped the floorplan with a finger. "Did you notice the moveable panel in the wall next to your fireplace? It appears to be another entrance to the passageway, albeit narrower than any of the others."

"Indeed? No, I hadn't realized it was there. What was the purpose, do you suppose? A priest's hole?"

His moustache lifted when he smiled. "I hardly think so. The house does not date back that far. More than likely it was intended as secret access to or from an assignation."

"I wonder how one releases the secret door?"

"Planning a rendezvous are you, my lady?"

She smiled at his obvious jest, then sobered. The nerve of the man! "You seem to find the idea somehow preposterous?"

"Not preposterous, Lady Udora, but certainly not your style. Correct me if I am wrong, but you seem to be the sort of woman who would not stoop to hide her dalliances behind closed doors."

She froze him with an icy warning. "You misstep yourself, sir. I never dally."

"Ah, yes. You mentioned your two marriages."

It seemed to Udora that he was probing her. Had someone been discussing her personal affairs with

Aaron Bently? Ridiculous! Who would dare? It was no business of his that she had wed, bedded and buried four men. Nor was it any concern of his that she had remained faithful, preferring to have each of her marriages blessed by the church. That wasn't to say she hadn't had far more than her share of flirtations. Indeed, some of them were quite... The memory brought a flush to her face.

Bently made no attempt to conceal his pleasure at her embarrassment. Why she chose to deal in half-truths was still a puzzle to him. But, he conceded with a slow smile, a puzzle which continued to give him the advantage over her. It was just a matter of time before he would be forced to make use of what he knew. Until then, he would savour the suspense like a child savours a piece of peppermint candy on Christmas Eve.

Udora snatched the floorplans from the table. "If you can spare the time, Mr. Bently, I would like you to show me this hidden entrance to the passageway."

He bowed. "If you will lead the way."

She started toward the door, then turned abruptly. "You realize all that we have discussed must be held in the strictest of confidences?"

"As you wish." He followed her down the long corridor and up the back stairs to the floor above. Dulcey and the new servant girl, Tilly, chose that moment to pass by and look up at them. They stopped and stared, mouths agape.

Udora pointed her finger. "Have you nothing else to do with your time? I've asked Mr. Bently to see to the crack in the upstairs banister railing. Now do get on with your own work."

Bently contrived to appear serious indeed when they reached the upstairs landing. "Is it the railing or the upright which is cracked, Lady Udora?"

"Oh, don't be a nick ninny. You know full well that it was merely a ruse to slake their curiosity. Otherwise the whole village would be talking about my having taken you into my bedchamber." She opened the door to her suite, then stepped back in surpise. Maggie was in the process of putting a fresh coverlet on the bed. Her eyes widened in shock.

"M'lady!"

"Oh, pistachions!" Udora said. "I thought you were belowstairs in the laundry."

"Yes, ma'am. I kin see that. Do you want me to make myself scarce like?"

"No. Of course not." She threw the roll of pressed paper on the bed with a sigh of frustration. "Yes. I think perhaps it might be better if you would. I have some things I wish to discuss with Mr. Bently in private."

Maggie looked from one to the other as a toothy grin spread across her face. For once she seemed to be caught without a saucy sally. She dropped a quick curtsy and scurried from the room, closing the door after her. They could hear her laughter as she ran towards the stairs.

Bently leaned indolently against the mantelpiece. "I wouldn't be too surprised if word gets out anyway, m'lady. One can't keep a tasty morsel like this away from the villagers."

"Tasty morsel, indeed. I'm sure I have no idea to what you refer."

He grinned. "I stand corrected."

"To be sure. Now if you would be so good as to show me how to open the passageway, you'll be free to return to your work."

He straightened and stroked his chin with his fingers. "Nothing would please me more, Lady Udora; however, that was the one detail which the architect saw fit to omit from the floorplans. We know where the door should be but we can only guess as to how to open it."

She approached the fireplace, removed a framed watercolour and ran her fingers along the mouldings. "How difficult can it be to locate?"

"The device which releases the door can be anywhere on this entire wall. I seriously doubt that it would be found in so obvious a place as the moulding, but I suppose I can try."

Moving aside so that he could explore the surface with his hands, Udora took the opportunity to observe his fine physique. The fabric of his shirt drawn tightly across his shoulders and back brought into focus the play of muscles strengthened by hard labour. The strong shoulders and back tapered down to a narrow waist and granite thighs.

She closed her eyes for an instant and when she opened them, Bently was observing her face. She grabbed a lace handkerchief from her bodice and dabbed at her eyes. "It's nothing. A bit of dust, I think."

He had the grace to remain silent, though his eyes spoke volumes. She challenged him with her gaze. "Well . . . have you found it?"

"Not yet. It's probably hidden near the damper just inside the fireplace."

"It seems silly to put it where one could easily get burned. Suffice to say the only sensible place would be the moulding."

Bently tapped the walls and tapped again. "I've no doubt that there *is* a passageway behind the wall, but I see nothing to prove that the doorway actually exists," he said as he straightened, favouring his left leg.

"I know it exists. I can feel it in my bones. We can't give up so easily."

"Another day, perhaps. It's growing late and I must return home."

"Pistachions! I dislike this nonsense of sharing you with Partridge Run when you're needed much more here."

"Are you suggesting that I take up residence at Amberleigh?"

"It appears the idea has crossed *your* mind." She reached up to rehang the painting but when the frame hit the nail it pushed downwards and the hidden doorway flew open. Udora was thrown backwards up against Bently, causing them to fall in a tangled heap on the floor.

At that moment they heard someone rapping at the door. Udora gasped. "Well, don't just lie there! Help me up!"

"There is no need to be alarmed. I took the precaution of locking the door."

"You did what?"

"You said you wished the panel to remain a secret. It seemed prudent..."

"Oh, do be still. And do get off me."

"I can't move, my lady. I fear I've gone numb."

"Oh. I'm so sorry. Have I injured your leg?"

"My leg is not the problem."

"I... oh."

Maggie rapped once more at the bedchamber door. "Is you all right, m'lady? I thought I 'eard a thump."

"It... it's nothing. Mr. Bently is helping me rearrange the furniture. Go down to the kitchen and fetch a broom."

"A broom? Me? 'Tis the new girl what does the sweepin' up."

"Just do as I tell you."

They heard her grumbling all the way down the hall. Bently leaned up on one elbow, a quizzical expression lighting his eyes. "I fear you have been thoroughly compromised, Lady Udora."

She sucked in her breath as the warmth of his own breath feathered her hair across her brow. "Don't be absurd. It...it was an accident. That's all." Her voice sounded breathy and husky, even to her own ears.

He bent his head closer. "A convenient one, wouldn't you agree?" Before she could respond he captured her chin in his free hand and kissed her expertly on the mouth.

When she finally gained sufficient control of her wayward emotions to pull away, she put her hand to her mouth, lest he see how she trembled. "How dare you, sir! You are no gentleman."

"On the contrary. No gentleman would refuse a lady when she goes to such extremes as to wrestle him onto the floor."

"I... oh! Get off me."

"But it's you who are on top."

"Then help me up."

"Of course. If that is what you really wish. As for myself, I found this interlude somewhat pleasant." He looked so satisfied with himself that Udora could not help but laugh.

"Aaron Bently, if you speak of this to a single soul I will have your guts for garters! And what do you mean, 'somewhat pleasant'? You couldn't have enjoyed yourself more if you'd planned it in advance."

"Possibly. It's something to consider for next time, however." He rolled her over on the floor and with some consideration to his lame leg and various other parts of his anatomy, managed to rise and lift her to her feet. "Your abigail is approaching. I suggest we close the hidden doorway if you wish it to remain a secret."

"Yes. We must. It wouldn't do for every Tom, Dick and Harry to know about it."

He was able to close the spring lock and rehang the painting at the precise moment that Udora unbolted the bedchamber door.

Maggie, holding the offending broom in front of her, looked around. "And wot 'appened to the furniture?"

"What do you mean what happened?" Udora asked in alarm.

"You said you were moving it about? It looks the same to me."

"Oh, that. It happened that I didn't like the arrangement and I simply asked Mr. Bently to move it back," Udora said, thinking fast.

"Yes, ma'am. Put it in the exact same spot, 'e did. Not even a single mark on the rug." Maggie, wearing her familiar smug expression, leaned the broom against the mantel.

"That will be all, Maggie."

"Yes, ma'am." She knew when she was being dismissed but she couldn't resist one last hit. "Will you be needin' me to 'elp with the curlin' tongs?"

Udora stole a glance in the mirror and was appalled by the state her hair was in. She stiffened. "No thank you. I'll ring for you if I have need of you."

"Yes, m'lady." Maggie giggled and closed the door behind her.

"Now see what you've done, Mr. Bently. We'll be the talk of the entire countryside."

"You can be sure of that, my lady." He turned to fix her with his gaze. A smile twitched the corners of his moustache, but when he spoke, there was a deep resonance to his voice which belied his jest. It was, however, his words which shook Udora's composure.

"I am nothing if not a gentleman, my lady. Since you are certain to have been compromised, please allow me to do the done thing and offer my hand in marriage."

"Marriage! To you?" Udora found that her hands were shaking. She was about to give him the setdown he deserved for such impudence, when he reached for her hands and held them between his palms. For a moment she thought he might kiss her again but he let her go.

She struggled to still the tremor in her voice. "Your offer is most considerate, Mr. Bently, but I could not, in good conscience, put you under such an obligation. I have endured censure in the past. I will also survive this time."

"As you wish. Then perhaps we should go belowstairs before the servants start to empty the bag."

Once again Bently was taking control, but somehow Udora didn't mind. She told him to return to his work while she repaired the damage to her hair. The dressing table mirror revealed more than she wanted to know. Her face was flushed and her eyes sparkled with excitement. As she rescued the pins in her hair, it occurred to her that one kiss from Bently was all it required to make her go soft in the head. She who had been courted by legions!

And who was he, anyway, but a country bumpkin...with the body of a devil and the eyes of a saint, she amended, knowing full well the risk involved if she continued to think of him in such terms.

And how could she be so fickle as to enjoy a flirtation when poor Charles must still be mourning their broken engagement? Charles was such a pet. She cared for him. And to even contemplate comparing her affection for him to what she was feeling for Bently was just short of sacrilege. Aaron Bently was so... She stumbled about in her brain for a word which would adequately describe him. Stubborn, bossy, proud, impertinent. Then remembering his brief but compelling kiss, she closed her eyes and whispered a very different description. "Healthy, handsome, strong, virile and very, very enticing." A man few women could resist. Thank heaven that she herself was a woman of experience who would not easily succumb to temptation. She laid the comb on the dressing table and took one last look in the mirror. The blush of passion had left her face. Odd how easy it had been to gain control once Bently had left the room.

ALSO, ON THE SUBJECT OF control, Udora realized that the time had come for her to assert her authority over the girls. And tonight was not too soon to put her plan into motion.

Everything was in readiness. Maggie, an unwilling accomplice, kept looking at the clock and grumbling about the needlework Udora had provided her with to keep her busy.

Finally Udora laid aside the feather hat she was repairing and fixed her abigail with a steady gaze. "What is it, Maggie? You're as restless as a hound at the start of a hunt. Could it be that you were thinking to meet someone?"

Maggie blushed. "Now 'oo would I be meetin' in this 'ere dratted cornfield?"

"Oh, I don't know." Udora's suspicious glance slid sideways. "The gamekeeper from Partridge Run, perhaps?"

Maggie sucked in her breath. "Blimey! An wot bigmouth rustic's been speakin' out o' turn? Was it that new girl? The one with the bowed legs and buck teeth?"

"Tut-tut. Such language. I really think you ought to be more careful of—" She stopped in mid-sentence and held a finger to her lips. "Hush. There it is, the rustling in the wall. Listen."

Maggie listened, her shoe-button eyes agate bright, her hands clutching the arms of the chair. She whispered. "I was right. There's a ghost wot walks in them walls. Iffen my legs weren't all o' jelly I'd get up and run."

"Nonsense. Be silent. They're coming closer."

"They? You mean there's more than one?"

"I'll wager there are three." She was about to elaborate when the air was rent by a low moan, which grew in intensity and was soon joined by another voice. Udora stepped up to the wall and removed the painting over the mantlepiece.

Maggie blanched. "Banshees straight from 'ell, they is comin' to git us m'lady."

Udora listened until the moans were coming from directly in front of her. In one quick move she pulled the nail downward and the panel swung open to reveal the three startled girls.

Udora pressed her hands together. "Oh, my dears. I heard your moans. Was it the pigeon pie or the roast quail that caused you such discomfort? Cook will be crushed." She held the secret panel open and waved all three inside. "Just be seated girls and I'll see if I can find some mineral salts to ease the pain." Then turning her back to them she closed the panel, taking care that they did not see how the device was sprung.

Maggie stared in bewilderment until Udora instructed her to add some fresh kindling to the fire. Then Udora turned to the girls. "Perhaps is it not salts you require, my dears. I have a notion you would all feel much better in your new gowns. So, come. Off with your clothes and be quick about it."

Taz was outraged. "We'll do no such thing and you can't make us. We'll go back to our own rooms." She stomped over to the bedchamber door but found it locked. Then she went to the fireplace and felt along the moulding for the secret panel.

"It's of no use, Topaz. You will remain here until *I* say you may go."

"Then I will stay here forever."

"Not wearing *that* dress you won't. You are no longer in mourning and can throw off your drabs. Miss Leavesly stitched up three lovely gowns for each of you. I'm sure you can find one that you like." She turned to the other girls who were already discarding their dresses. "Good. You look much improved already. Taz, if you cannot manage, Maggie and I will be happy to assist you."

"If you touch me I'll squeak beef," Taz said, but she began undoing the multitude of rusty buttons which held the drab dress together.

When they had all disrobed, Udora took the dresses and fed them to the fire. "Now then, Maggie, let's see if we can't find something comfortable for the girls to put on while we share a pot of chocolate and some of Cook's cinnamon jumbles."

Maggie went to the armoire and brought out three gaily wrapped parcels, which she then handed to the girls. Udora seated herself in a chair across from the bed upon which all three girls sat. "Go on, open them. It's a little something I sent for from London. I've been saving them for a special occasion."

Amy had unwrapped hers first and was fingering the figured silk.

"What is it?" she asked. "It feels so soft."

Emmy pushed her spectacles back up her nose. "It's a Japanese kimono, silly. I've seen pictures of them in my books. Are they really for us?"

Udora picked up the wrapping and folded it into a neat square. "Of course they are." She dimpled. "The lilac is for Amethyst, the green for you, Emerald, and the pale gold is for Topaz. But I wouldn't advise crawling about the walls while wearing them. The fabric is imported silk."

Amy fastened her kimono round her waist and whirled about the room. "It makes me feel like a princess."

Taz was scornful. "Princesses don't bite their nails." She looked over at Emmy. "And they don't wear ugly spectacles, either."

Em appeared hurt but deliberately picked up a book from Udora's table and sank down casually into a chair. Amy, looking defiant, hid her hands in the voluminous sleeves of her kimono but was sufficiently cowed by Topaz to avoid a rejoinder.

Udora hugged Amy. "Never mind, child. We know that Topaz only meant to be helpful. So why don't we repay her the kindness."

They all three snapped to attention. Topaz's response was wary. "I don't choose to be repaid, thank you."

"Come now, Topaz. Kindness is as kindness does. Sit down, child. By the dressing table. This may take a while, but young ladies as well as princesses would not be caught out of bed without their hair brushed. From now on you will brush it fifty strokes each day, but just this once, I'll do it for you."

Topaz was frantic for some avenue of escape, but when she found none, she resigned herself to the situation. "You can try but you shall not get far. Cleverer people than you have tried to brush it and gave up."

"We'll see, won't we?"

Udora fastened a cloth round Taz's shoulders to protect her kimono, then applied a dab of oily lotion, which Maggie had heated over the lamp, to her hair. Taz recoiled. "Ugh. What is that? It smells nasty."

"A special oil made from, uh, made to soften dry hair. Sit still. I promise this is going to work wonders."

The twins watched in fascination as Udora brushed through the snarls inch by inch. By the expression on their faces she guessed that this was the first time Topaz had been forced to do something against her will. Maggie, who detested "the one wi' the smart mouth," as she always called her, was enjoying every minute. Particularly when she saw a tear run down Taz's cheek and onto her lap. Taz refused to cry out, even when the snarls pulled their worst. Nor would she admit to her tears by wiping them away. Udora's heart went out to her. It was like seeing herself as a child on the verge of womanhood, growing up in a house where tears were viewed as weakness. And weakness was a sign of failure.

Moreover, she guessed, part of Topaz's ill-nature stemmed from the fact that she was not one of the twins and, in truth, was adopted.

When Udora was finished she pulled Topaz to her feet and gave her a hug. "There now. You look as pretty as any young lady of the ton."

"And I smell like a stable."

Maggie snorted. "Nothin's changed, then."

Amy, lying on her stomach on the bed, leaned up on her elbows and stared. "You look so beautiful, Taz. Your hair . . . it shines like spun gold."

Em looked up from her book and shook her head. "No. It is more the colour of flax drying in the sun, but it does smell quite dreadful, doesn't it? Like sheep's wool left in the rain."

She was deliberately baiting Taz and Udora shot her a warning glance. "I have the perfect solution, so to speak." Taking a glass perfume bottle from the dressing table, she sprinkled a generous amount of Attar of Roses on Topaz's hair.

Taz sneezed. "Smelling like a stable was better than this!"

"Don't be a cabbagehead, child. The perfume cost—" A noise emanating from the wall next to the fireplace stopped midsentence. It was a dry, papery sound not unlike the rustling the girls had made when they crept through the secret passageway.

Maggie's face turned white. "Lord o' mercy! If there's three o' them 'ere, 'ho's that in the wall?"

All five women dove for the bed and pulled the blanket up over their heads.

CHAPTER SEVEN

THOUGH UDORA'S BED was capacious, it was nevertheless very crowded. In the semi-darkness beneath the quilt, Udora gave Topaz a speaking look. "If this is another of your clever little rigs I'll pack you off to board-school."

Topaz shook her head. "It isn't, not this time. You must believe me."

Observing the tenseness around her mouth, Udora was convinced. "Very well, but if you had naught to do with it, then who or what is it?"

Em, still searching for the spectacles which fell from her nose in the commotion, squinted up at Udora. "You're the guardian. You're supposed to tell *us*!"

"Don't be impertinent, Emerald."

Amy moved closer to Udora. "I think it's shaking the bed. I'm scared, Lady Udora. What are we going to do?"

Udora peeked out just long enough to ascertain that the panel remained closed. She glanced round for Maggie, who was hidden under the blanket at the far end of the bed. Udora laughed. "It's Maggie who's shaking the bed. Take hold of yourself, girl, before you have us all in a jim-jam."

"And weren't it I said wot this 'ouse was 'aunted, m'lady. You've brung us to our doom this time, you 'ave."

"Do be still," Udora commanded. "Listen. The sound has ceased and we've been behaving like shatter-brains. It's time we found out what this is all about."

Maggie wrapped her fingers round the bedpost. "Don't be lookin' at me, m'lady."

Udora took a deep breath and gathered her courage. When her feet touched the floor she felt a brush against her ankle. She pulled back quickly but not before something swooshed past her ear and landed on her shoulder. Udora screeched as the hairy black spider fell to the floor.

Taz crawled out from under the blanket and picked up the offending creature. She looked contrite. "This time it *is* my fault but not the others."

Udora stared at the spider. Paper. Nought but black paper trimmed with bits of black hair and red glass eyes which seemed to glow in the lamplight. Udora shuddered. "I detest spiders."

"I know. I—I saw you run from one one day in the garden."

"Observant of you," Udora said drily. "How did you manage to make it fall in just the right place?"

"I—I tied a thread to your bedpost. Then I went up to the roof and tied the middle of the string to the window which opens in the dome. The other end I tied to the spider. When you broke the thread the spider fell."

"Ingenious, I must admit, and artistic, too. But there will be no more crawling on the roof. Am I understood? And no more spiders, please."

"Yes, ma'am." Taz looked genuinely frightened. "But there's still that noise in the wall. I swear we had nothing to do with it."

Amy pushed the cover back from her head. "P'raps we should leave it be. Maybe it'll go away."

Udora laughed. "I doubt that, child. Besides, I'm not afraid of ghosts, at least not when compared to spiders. Stay where you are, all of you and I will see to our intruder."

Typically, Taz ignored instructions and followed her over to the wall. Udora studied her with obvious disapproval then shrugged, handed her the watercolour to hold and motioned for her to stand aside. Breathing a silent prayer, Udora pulled down on the nail and the panel swung outward.

Four pairs of red eyes glowed in the lamplight. All five women gasped. But then Udora laughed, for when the dust cleared, her cats filed out. "Shame on you, boys." Udora sounded a bit hysterical but she managed to gain control. "Have you lost your manners scaring us like that?"

Ulysses and Odysseus, the tabby twins, curled up on the rug next to the fireplace. Prometheus and Telemachus, who switched his reddish-brown tail as if to demonstrate his disdain, both hopped up onto the bed where they were welcomed by Amy and Em. Maggie tossed the coverlet back and struggled out of bed.

"Them blasted cats is goin' to be cat stew one o' these foin days."

"Mind your language, my girl." Udora pressed her hands together and sighed. "Now isn't this cozy? The room is all toasty and the fire is banked. The bed is big enough for everyone. Why don't you girls stay with me tonight? Just for tonight, mind. We can chat and tell stories and eat cinnamon jumbles in the dark."

Amy's eyes sparkled. "Can the cats stay too?"

"Of course. This is their home."

There was silence for a moment as the three girls looked at one another. Then Em spoke. "Does this mean you won't leave us like all the others did?"

"I'll remain here for as long as you have need of me. This is my home, as well now, my dear child."

"And what about...'Charles, my pet,'" Topaz asked, giving a poor but accurate imitation of Udora.

Udora hesitated, then put her arm round Taz. "You needn't worry, sweetling. All is quite finished between Mr. Willingsly and me. Charles is young and eligible. He will soon find someone else, unless I miss my guess."

Em, having found her spectacles which were caught between the pillows, replaced them on her nose. "And does the same thing apply to you, Lady Udora? You aren't exactly past prayin' for. What if you find someone else? Will you leave us then?"

"Rest assured, girls, I'm not looking for someone else."

Maggie snorted and spoke from the doorway. "Not much you ain't." Udora looked daggers at her before the girl sashayed into her own room.

Long after the hot chocolate and the cinnamon jumbles ran out, Udora continued to regale the girls with stories of her days at board-school. When they tired of them she talked about the London Season and what it was like to make your bow before the Regent. And the dances at Almack's and the parties that she and Yvette had hosted at The Lark's Nest.

Amy was the first to fall asleep, then Em and finally Taz. Udora turned on her side to study their profiles, so sweet, so innocent, so vulnerable as they slept.

Sandwiched in between girls and cats, Udora gazed up at the golden dome which gave Amberleigh its name and for the first time she was truly grateful that she had inherited the Thackery Jewels. Ulysses stretched his forelegs then flattened his ears as he jumped onto the bed next to Udora. She reached over to scratch his chin. He purred and in the faint glow from the fire, they exchanged looks of utter contentment.

IT WAS JUST AFTER SIX the next morning when they were awakened by someone pounding on the front door. Udora untangled herself from the twist of cats and girls and went to the window. There was a horse tied at the post but the entryway was beyond her line of vision. She pulled on a robe and went into the hallway, but McMasters had already responded to the urgent summons and was starting up the stairway to speak to her.

"What is it, McMasters?" she asked, at the same time taking note of his carefully groomed appearance. Vaguely, she wondered if he slept without moving so as to avoid becoming mussed.

"It's a fire, my lady. In the granary, I believe. The farmers are already working to extinguish it."

"Indeed! I must go there at once."

"I hardly think it necessary." He made it seem like an everyday occurence.

"Nonsense. Have the groom saddle a horse for me immediately."

"Yes, my lady."

Taz and the twins were awake when Udora returned to her room and Maggie had already laid out a fresh camisole and a riding costume. "Good girl," Udora said, then told them about the fire.

Maggie yawned. "Does you want I should come wi' you?"

"No. It won't be necessary."

Taz scrambled from the bed. "I'm coming."

"No. You girls stay here. I will return as soon as possible."

Amy, Em and the cats were still in bed when she left with the groom to show her the way. Taz had gone to her own room.

When Udora and the groom reined up a short distance from the scene of the fire, Taz, dressed in a riding costume that was three sizes too large for her, was tying her horse to a post. Udora heaved a sigh. "I thought I told you to stay home."

Taz shrugged. "The fire is nearly out. I wanted to see what was happening."

"I understand but you should not have come unescorted. It isn't ladylike."

Udora saw that one end of the building was almost completely destroyed, but a bucket brigade of farm workers from Amberleigh and Partridge Run had kept the fire from spreading. The immediate danger had passed.

The groom helped Udora dismount. Udora questioned him. "Have you heard if anyone was hurt?"

"No, mum, I don't think so."

"How did it start? Does anyone know?"

"Old Simon was up with his rheumatics when 'e says 'e saw a man runnin' from the barn. That and the smell o' whale oil makes them think 'twas set, purposelike."

Udora saw that Topaz was wearing only a thin shawl. She removed her own cape and wrapped it round the girl's shoulders. "Do hold still. You'll catch your death if you take a chill. I'm far too warm with my heavy shawl and a woolen dress, as well." She spotted Bently silhouetted against the red haze of the dying fire. "I wish to speak to Mr. Bently before I return, Topaz. The groom will see you safely back to the house."

Taz hesitated. "There's something I need to tell you, Lady Udora."

"Yes, dear, what is it?"

"We should have told you from the start but everyone—"

Udora stopped her when she saw Bently coming towards them. She patted Taz's arm. "We'll have a nice long chat a bit later. Right now it's very important that I speak to Mr. Bently."

Taz looked annoyed, then yanked at the ribbons and mounted her horse in one smooth motion. The cloak fell to the ground in a heap, a gesture of disdain which spoke more eloquently than words. As she spun the horse in the direction of the main house, Taz called something over her shoulder but Udora could only catch the first word. "Lord . . ." Something. The rest if it was lost in the commotion of the fire and the pounding of horses' hooves as the groom followed after her.

Bently dismounted next to Udora, who was obviously appalled. "Was that profanity Taz was using just then?"

Bently seemed to tense. "You didn't hear her?" His voice was bland. "Then I wouldn't be concerned. Taz rarely indulges in profanity."

"What of the fire? Was it deliberately set, as my groom overheard someone suggest?"

"Yes. You can be assured of that. I suspect Dodson, although I have no proof."

"Isn't it proof enough that he threatened revenge for being discharged?"

"Not without evidence. The fire is under control now and the damage is not as severe as it may appear. There is nothing here that you can do," he said, standing so close that she could see the glow of the fire reflected in his eyes. In his hurry to dress he wore no coat and had left the top buttons of his shirt undone, revealing a dark V of chest hair.

Udora's voice was husky. "I suppose I should leave, just to be certain that Taz returned safely. She was angry again."

"Taz is always angry." He picked up the cloak and wrapped it round Udora's shoulders. His hands remained at her collar for what seemed like an eternity as their gaze met and held. She lifted her chin and closed her eyes, for surely it was his intention to kiss her. But maddeningly, he simply cleared his throat.

"I mustn't keep you, my lady." His hands captured hers where they had somehow found their way to rest on his chest. She heard him chuckle. "Since you so quickly turned down my proposal of marriage, I cannot allow myself to further compromise your reputation."

Devil take the man. How dare he reject her? She swore silently, knowing that he was fully awake to the fact that she was not yet ready to release him. She turned her hand in his and reached to stroke the square line of his jaw. He groaned and pulled her close. His mouth was inches away from hers.

With considerable difficulty she drew back. Her voice was ragged. "Ah, yes, Mr. Bently. Suffice to say, you are correct, as always. We must not flout Polite Society."

His chest was heaving. When he could finally speak clearly he tried to pull her once again into the circle of his arms. "My dear Lady Udora. It does occur to me that we are rather far removed from the dictates of London Society at this moment."

She stepped back, savouring her triumph despite the toll it had taken on her to do so. "Even so, Mr. Bently, I hadn't realized how late it is. If you will be so good as to help me mount my horse, I shall allow you to escort me back to the house."

She heard him suck in his breath. "What is it you were going to say, Mr. Bently?"

"Nothing, my lady. Not a bloody thing."

Point made! she thought. But the victory was far less satisfying than she had anticipated.

IN THE DAYS which followed, every effort was made to find Dodson and extract an admission from him that he had set the fire in the granary, but it was as if he had vanished. It was several days before Udora could convince herself that he was no longer a threat to them.

That night before the fire had, however, signified a turning point in her relationship with the girls. Bently remarked on it one morning when Udora placed a small stack of bills on his worktable.

He thumbed through them and looked up. "A definite improvement, I'd say. We've managed to cut our expenditures while at the same time increasing production. The lambing will begin soon, and then we must start to think seriously about the condition of the fields."

"The credit goes to you, Mr. Bently. You've worked wonders with the farm . . . and with the farm families. They speak highly of you."

"And of you," he interjected. "Everyone says that you've turned those three wild hell-cats into bewitching young ladies."

"Hardly ladies," Udora said with a laugh. "But they are coming along quite well. At least they are beginning to look the part. If only I could instill in each of them a sense of decorum."

"They know how to go on in Polite Society."

Udora tilted her head to one side. "It takes more than knowing. It must become second nature to them so that they automatically do the proper thing."

"Then I suppose you must take them to London for the Season. Will you attempt to fire them off this year?"

Udora was appalled. "That would be a disaster. Besides, they are a bit too young. I would like to see them turn sixteen before they make their bow to the Regent."

"Does that mean you will forgo the Season this year?" he asked, regarding her closely. He was not prepared for the wistful expression which darkened her eyes.

She walked to the window and drew the drapery aside. "I suppose I must. And it's going to be such a splendid Season. The list of balls and parties grows by the day. I understand that Lord and Lady Frogmartin are returning from the Indies and will open their new house in Mayfair for a magnificent soirée. I can't begin to tell you of the marvellous things which are planned this Season."

The afternoon sun coming through the window made a halo around her hair, turning it to red gold. He rose and walked over to stand near her, making sure to maintain a respectful distance. "It is still a few weeks before the Season begins. The girls have been left in the care of servants in the past. You could take some time away from Amberleigh to attend some of the parties. Everyone knows how very much you deserve it."

"And leave them just when they need me most? I couldn't possibly do that. In truth, it is only since I convinced them that I would not desert them that they have come to trust me." She let the drapery fall and the room was once again in shadow. "No. The Season is out of the question."

He could almost feel her disappointment. "It means so much to you, does it?"

She nodded. "Silly, isn't it? But I miss my friends and the music and dancing. Ah, yes, the dancing. The girls would love the parties and the excitement of seeing the great town houses and the ladies dressed in all their finery. But alas, I could never have them made presentable in time for the Season's opening." She stopped suddenly. "But of course there is the Little Season. They will have turned sixteen by then." She gazed at him with all the delight of a babe with its first sweet. "Why ever didn't I think of it before?"

He smiled at her unexpected giddiness. "August, a good few months away. By then you will surely have the girls behaving like princesses."

Udora laughed. "I'll be content if they can carry on a decent conversation and make an acceptable curtsy." She clasped her hands together. "I know just the thing. Before the rush to London begins, we'll have a party and send invitations to all the great country houses from Coventry to London."

Her hands flew to her face. "Pistachions! Whatever shall I do for an escort?" She dimpled. "Perhaps I should choose you, Mr. Bently. That would give the gossips something to twitter about, don't you think?"

His face sobered and Udora detected a desperate look in his eyes. "There is something I've been wanting to tell you, Lady Udora."

"Indeed, and just what—" At that moment Amy burst into the room. "My lady, come see. Tom is putting the sailboat in the river. Taz and Em are there, too. We're going for a sail."

"Oh, dear! That will never do. It's far too dangerous."

Amy looked deflated. "It isn't, really. We've always taken the boat out by ourselves." She looked her most appealing. "Tell her it's true, my lord."

Aaron's face clouded for an instant before he met Udora's gaze. His eyes were dark and fathomless. "It's true. The girls have been using the boat without supervision since the year before their parents passed on."

"But the river is so wide and the water is so high."

"Yes, indeed, and the boat has been hauled for the winter. Perhaps I should see to its soundness before it's put in the water."

"But we wish to use it now," Amy protested, catching his hand and looking up at him in so bewitching a way that Udora could have sworn the girl was flirting.

Aaron Bently patted her cheek. "Then I shall look at it now, little one."

Udora chuckled. "And I shall accompany you. I've always been partial to sailboats. My father taught me to sail when I was but five years old."

Bently, appearing extraordinarily pleased, gave Amy a push. "Run out to the stable, child, and ask Blodgett to bring round the gig. Then run down to the river and tell Tom not to put the boat in the water until I've had a chance to determine that it's safe."

Amy scurried off, eyes bright, curls bouncing.

Udora shook her head. "You realize, don't you, Mr. Bently, that they sent Amethyst because she is so winsome that no one could possibly refuse her?"

He inclined his head. "You are learning their ways very quickly, my lady."

"But not as quickly as I would like," she mused. It occurred to her that something Amy said had stuck in the back of her mind and wouldn't come forward. She concentrated for a moment but when Bently's expression became inquisitive, she shrugged. "It's Topaz who worries me. She is so clever and so... so unpredictably daring."

A slow smile lighted his eyes. "Not entirely unlike you, my lady. Am I not right?"

"I fear that you are correct, Mr. Bently. And that is what concerns me. I was known to go to the mischief in my time."

He seemed to study her from head to foot until the colour rose in her face and she had to look away. His laughter sent a wave of heat coursing through her. "One could never claim that you turned out less than remarkable, Lady Udora. For years you've had London Society at your feet not to mention two marriages to—"

She cut him short. "You embarrass me, sir. Perhaps we should be watching for the gig." Much as she wanted to, Udora could not bring herself to admit that she had made four, not two, marches down the matrimonial aisle. Truth be told, it was none of his affair, but it irked her to dissemble. She cudgeled her brain for a change of subject.

"I believe you had something you wished to discuss with me before Amy burst in upon us."

He stroked his chin. Confound it. He had the words written down in his mind in just the way he wanted to say them, but they had vanished along with the moment. It was important that he acquit himself well or he would lose whatever chance he had with her. He limped over to the window. "Yes, there was something, but another time, perhaps. I hear the gig coming round to the front. Shall I fetch you a cape?"

THE SAILBOAT was hardly large enough for the three girls, but Aaron judged it to be seaworthy. Although there was a slow-moving current and a steady breeze, Bently said the girls, all three of whom could swim, would be quite safe. The river was wide, but Bently pointed out that the small wooded island, a few hundred yards offshore, would offer some protection from unexpected wind gusts.

Udora pressed her palms together. "Nevertheless, I'd feel ever so much better if we could see them from the shore."

"Shall we drive along the river road towards Partridge Run? You've hardly seen that part of the estate since you arrived."

"I'd like that. Perhaps sometime you would also show me round Partridge Run...with your master's permission, of course."

He smiled and slapped the reins against the horse's flank. "Whenever you wish, Lady Udora. As I said before, I am my own master." He drew a deep breath. "If truth be told—"

She put her hand on his arm. "Yes...yes, of course. Look, there they are rounding the bend. Is that Topaz at the tiller?"

Bently sighed. "Rest assured it would have to be Topaz. Neither Em nor Amy would be given the chance to steer. Taz always needs to be the one who controls things."

"I've noticed that. The other girls are more inclined to accept my guardianship, but Taz has yet to yield her will to my supervision."

He was silent as he turned the horse towards a bridge which forded a small, swift-running stream. "It is early days yet to expect a complete conversion. Taz is a highly intelligent child and it would be sad indeed to squelch her spirit."

"Indeed." Udora was thoughtful. "The girl knows she's adopted. Does she know the identity of her true parents?"

He seemed to hesitate overlong. "I hardly think so," he said at last.

Udora shot him a quizzical look. "And do you, Bently?"

He blanched. "I have my suspicions, but mind, they are only that and I would not care to share them for fear that they are in error."

Udora had to be content with that, but it would not have surprised her if Aaron Bently himself had a significant connection. Few women could resist the spell he cast without so much as a single effort on his part.

The thought of him lying with another woman was enough to take the wind out of her sails. Allowing her gaze to travel from the boat on the river to a copse nestled along the hillside leading into a pleasant valley, Udora found that she needed to lift her spirits.

"Oh look," she cried. "What a truly lovely spot. How could I have failed to notice it the day I came looking for the girls at Partridge Run?"

"Most likely as a result of your distraught state of mind. The Thackerys called this section of the estate Deep Springs Park. The stream which we just crossed over has its source in the spring and it eventually feeds into the river.'' He pointed to a wooden tower on the far side of the ravine. ''The dovecote you see is at Partridge Run. Our property borders Deep Springs to the north.''

Udora saw, topping the crest of the hill, tall chimneys rising above slate roofs and stone walls broken at frequent intervals by leaded windows. ''It's lovely, isn't it? I've come to appreciate the country more than I ever thought possible. There is something so peaceful and simple about it.''

''The land will be yours one day, as I presume you know.''

''I beg your pardon. What are you saying?''

''Deep Springs Park. I assumed Mr. Watley had informed you that this small section of parkland would become yours as payment for having seen the girls through their marriage rituals.''

''I had no idea. I do remember something about being compensated for my efforts but I assumed it was to be a bauble...a bit of jewellery or porcelain to add to my collection.''

''Perhaps I shouldn't have told you. If so, I apologize for speaking out of turn.''

''How did you come upon the knowledge?''

''Quentin Thackery told me. I was witness to the signing of the will.'' He flicked the ribbons and the horse moved smartly forward. ''What will you do with the land once you inherit?''

''I have no idea. There is too much to be seen to and accomplished before then for me to be concerned with something which I didn't know even existed.''

As the gig rounded a bend in the road, she turned her head for one last look. "I wonder that your master could absent himself from here for so long. His concerns must be very engrossing to keep him from all this, but to do him credit, he has left the estate in remarkably capable hands." She adjusted her bonnet. "Now, much as I hate to, I fear I must return to supervise the girls. They have duties to attend to at the house."

Bently winced. Another moment to tell her had come and gone. He was caught in a maze constructed of his own deception, and he was left stumbling into corridors with no egress. He mumbled something indistinguishable over the clatter of hooves on gravel as he turned the horse and gig towards Amberleigh.

THE SAILBOAT REMAINED a major attraction for the girls for the next few days. Udora suspected that one of the reasons for their interest was to avoid the work involved in preparations for the house party. It was to last three days. Invitations had been delivered to noble houses for miles around. If truth be told, Udora had harboured a fear that she had not chosen convenient dates because far too many invitations had been returned with the senders' regrets. The range of excuses seemed plausable at first glance, but upon giving them honest consideration, Udora recognized the transparent ploys she had often used to avoid attending certain parties.

But it was too late to cancel plans. She had spent too much money and had become too involved with preparations to cry off now.

Udora placed a stack of bills on the table in Bently's workroom. "I must say, I'm somewhat disappointed by the lack of attention our party is receiving. I had thought the Thackery name, not to mention my own, might be better known in these parts."

Bently raised an eyebrow at the considerable number of bills, but he placed them in a drawer. "There was a time when Amberleigh was full of laughter and good cheer. But it has been several years since it has been opened to entertain. I'm sure it will take a little time for Society to recognize and remember the Thackery name."

Mrs. Kragen, who had been supervising the cleaning and dusting, and was therefore in a position where she had been privy to their conversation sniffed. "Time? I don't zink zo. Der are zose who zay zat to brink a husband to a party giffen by the beautiful vidow lady is like leading a gander to za chopping block."

Udora was appalled. "Surely you jest, Mrs. Kragen. They simply cannot be concerned that I would be so indiscriminate. I have only just broken my engagement."

"Ya, zat is just so."

"Yes, I see your point."

Bently consulted a calendar. "There are still a number of invitations to be returned. I'm sure the house will be full to overflowing. Don't you agree Mrs. Kragen?"

"Ya, m'lord. Ve vill haff music and dancink und ze house vill be full of laughter."

Just as Mrs. Kragen spoke Udora happened to intercept the warning look Bently directed to Mrs. Kragen.

She studied their faces. Something was afoot. The undercurrents of tension had been building for some time. Her mind still retained the bits and pieces of information which had never been put together. The half-finished sentences that Taz had begun when she left the fire so abruptly; the bit of dialogue that had slipped into Amy's conversation the first day of boating; the sly glances passed between the girls and Aaron Bently.

Udora thought back over what Mrs. Kragen had just said, and then it began to come clear. She felt the heat rise in her face and she strode from the room, slamming the door behind her.

CHAPTER EIGHT

RAGE, THAT'S WHAT IT WAS, Udora decided. How could he have done this to her? How could *they all* have done this to her? And, how many people knew of the deception? She strode into the rose garden, scarcely noticing the riot of blossoms nurtured by the gardner Bently had hired on to do the pruning. Did the girls know? Of course they knew. Everyone knew, including her own staff, most likely. Loyal as they were, they would never turn a deaf ear to kitchen gossip. How could she have been so blind?

Hearing a door close, Udora looked round to see Maggie walking down the kitchen garden path towards the stable. She called to her. "And where might you be going, miss? I thought you were told to mend my pelisse."

"'Tis mended and 'ung in the armoire next to your red cape, m'lady."

"Indeed, and was that the only thing which needed repair, or is it more important for you to run off to the barn to commit vagaries with that sapscull, Luther Jones?"

Maggie grinned. "Iffen I 'ad me choice..."

"Well, you do not," Udora snapped. "Not if you wish to remain in my employ."

Maggie raised her eyes to the sky. "Lord o' mercy, she be on 'er 'igh ropes."

"Silence. Tell me, Maggie. How long have you known that Aaron Bently is Lord Kesterson?"

Maggie looked momentarily stricken but recovered quickly. "No more 'n three days, my lady, I swear it. 'Twas Luther what told me when I told 'im as 'ow Mr. Bently was takin' a fancy to me." Seeing the look on her mistress's face, Maggie hastily added, " But once I learnt who Mr. Bently was, I knew 'e was above me touch, so I left 'im to you."

"How generous. And you chose not to tell me his true identity?"

"You didn't ask. An I knows 'ow you 'ates it when we gossips belowstairs," Maggie said, feigning innocence.

"Indeed." Udora gave her a quelling look. "Very well, then, since you are so good at keeping secrets, I want you to promise not to tell anyone that *I* know who Bently really is."

Maggie nodded vigorously. "Yes m'lady. You kin trust me not to say notin'."

"Yes, I believe I can, considering that I'll send you down to the scullery to wash dishes if you breathe one word of this to anyone."

"Yes m'lady. Is there anything else?"

"Not at the moment. You may go now but I advise you to watch your step from now on."

Maggie bobbed a curtsy, then turned to leave, but at the last minute she stopped and looked back. "But there is this one thing, m'lady. It does make it kinda nice for you, don't it? Him bein' a lord and all." Before Udora could respond, Maggie had disappeared round the end of the garden wall.

Udora yanked at a rosebud, pricking her finger in the process. Wiping the blood from her finger, she muttered an unladylike curse. This, too, was his fault. He had no right to deceive her. Or any reason, as far as she could see. One thing for certain. He would account for his deception and she would take pleasure in exacting her revenge.

She smiled at the thought, sobered, then smiled again. Pistachions! Maggie was right after all. It was *nice* knowing that Aaron Bently and Lord Kesterson were one and the same. It explained, if not simplified, her growing attraction for the man. She was not, after all, dangling after a country bumpkin. Her instincts had not failed her. She still recognized Quality when she saw it.

Not that she considered herself too grand to be attracted to a man of lower birth. After all, clear eyes, good muscles and teeth and a strong back were quite sufficient to turn any woman's head. And the addition of a title was a bonus into the bargain.

She threw the rose to the ground, then at the last minute stooped to pick it up and tuck it in the bosom of her gown. One problem was solved. She could be assured of a proper escort for the party as well as taking the arm of the most ruggedly handsome and virile man she had ever met.

Aaron Bently, watching her from the window of his office, saw that Udora was smiling. He ran his fingers around the top of his neckcloth and sighed. He was safe for yet another day, but soon, very soon he must find a way to tell her the truth about himself. He shifted his weight to his good leg. After the party, perhaps. That way he could avoid the inconvenience of acting as her escort.

He cursed the sabre wound which had so abruptly ended his service to the regent. It had also effectively put a period to the sort of life he had once enjoyed, for what woman would be content to sit out the whirl of the London Season? Udora herself had often mentioned her love of dancing. In the privacy of his own suite at Partridge Run he had tried to move to the music of the waltz, but to no avail. He was lame now, and lame he would always be, no matter how hard he tried to strengthen the muscles in his leg. He sighed. But he must try. He must never stop trying. Nor could he, now that he had fallen under Udora's spell.

Five minutes later when she returned to the library adjoining his workroom, Bently heard Udora humming. He breathed easier, hoping that whatever had tripped her temper was now forgotten. Nevertheless, he contrived to keep his distance until she approached him with business at hand.

IT HAD RAINED for nearly a week filling the river to the very top of its banks and keeping everyone indoors. Then, as if on demand from Udora, the sky cleared and the countryside became a sea of wildflowers. It became her daily habit to sail the small boat round the island each morning after an early breakfast. The girls, having tired of the boat, had at last taken an interest in dancing. Or was it the dancing instructor who interested them? Udora knew his limitations. Marcus Andulay was a clown, a travelling adventurer who had somehow managed to acquire a token knowledge of dancing skills. To be sure, it was not enough to prepare the girls for Almack's, but it was a start. And he delighted them. A little too much so, Udora sometimes thought, but she left the girls under the watchful eye of Maggie while she herself went sailing.

On one such morning Udora stopped in the workroom to speak with Bently. "You came early this morning, I see."

He rose in deference to her, and once more Udora was impressed by his natural grace despite his lame leg. Dressed in a claret-coloured coat, buff trousers and polished bulchers, he appeared groomed and freshly shaven.

He stood until she motioned him to sit. He inclined his head and resumed his place at the table. "Forgive me, my lady, if my early arrival disturbed the household. I wished to twice-check the estimated cost I prepared concerning the change to four-course rotation of the fodder crops."

"And are you still satisfied that it would be profitable to do so?"

"Admittedly it requires forward thinking, but Coke of Holkham has produced excellent results."

"Suffice to say that the duke is well versed in the latest methods of farming. I leave the decision to you." She settled a straw chip bonnet over her curls and tied it under her chin. "I'm off to the river for a sail. Why don't you come with me, Mr. Bently?"

He looked startled. "I say, I rather fancy the idea. But I thought you preferred the time alone. Are you certain you don't mind the company?"

Udora laughed. "When have I ever objected to your company? Fact of the matter is, there is something I wish to discuss with you."

"May I know what it is?"

"Later. I prefer to take the air before the sun becomes too strong."

He rose and motioned to the door. "After you, my lady."

The gig was already waiting to take them to the river. In less than a half-hour the sail was set against the wind and they were scudding downstream at a breathtaking clip. Udora leaned back onto a pillow, content to watch Bently handle the tiller. They were tacking round the southerly point of the island when Udora lifted the hem of her skirt.

"Pistachions! My gown is wet. We must be taking on water."

"Nonsense. We've plenty of freeboard. You must have dipped the hem of your skirt in the water when you came onboard."

"I tell you we are taking on water. Look, it's already over the ribs near the stern." Udora lifted her skirt above her boots. "Dear heaven, Mr. Bently. This is most serious. You've got to turn back."

It took only a second for him to realize that she was right. Water was seeping in faster than they could bale it out. He leaned the boat into the wind urging the sail to extend to its fullest but the added weight of the water slowed their progress.

"Perhaps I could help us along with the pole," Udora said.

"No. The water is too deep."

"We'll never make it to shore."

"I'm afraid you're right. It's too late to turn back, Lady Udora. We'll be swamped before we make a landing. I'll head for the island."

Their progress was excruciatingly slow as he tacked first one direction and then the other. At last they approached a nearly submerged wooden pier and as Bently dropped the sail, Udora tied the line to a post.

"Good work!" Bently said as he hoisted himself onto the dock Then took her hands to pull her up beside him. The winter storms had played havoc with the pier, leaving broken boards and railings cast askew or missing entirely in several places. Without another word, Bently scooped her into his arms and carried her onto dry land. Udora's arm had somehow found its way around his neck and it occurred to her that it seemed as natural as if it belonged there.

He put her down with considerable reluctance. His gaze met hers and held. He would have kissed her if he hadn't been so concerned about their circumstances. At best the island was a dry haven in the daytime, but it was also so isolated as to not even come to mind during the daily activity around the farm. His hands remained on her shoulders for more time than was proper but he was loath to let go of her.

Udora on the other hand, found it rather lowering of him to put her down without so much as a peck on the cheek, particularly when she had made her wishes quite obvious. At that precise moment she wished fervently that he were the country bumpkin she first believed. The dark-cloaked rider she first saw charging down out of the hills to challenge their carriage would have kissed her soundly, given such an opportunity. Bently had automatically reverted to being a gentleman, more's the pity, she thought. Courtly manners were fine in their place but this was hardly the place!

"What is it, Lady Udora?" he asked. "Are you frightened?"

"Of what?" she demanded, more amused than irritated. "Of you? I think not, Mr. Bently."

A gleam caught fire in his dark eyes. "Indeed. But perhaps you should be."

She lifted her chin. "Perhaps, sir, it is you who should be afraid of me. You forget with whom you are dealing."

"No. You misjudge me. I make it a rule to never underestimate my adversary."

"I was not aware that we are opponents, *Mr.* Bently. You are my employee, and I expect your complete honesty."

He hesitated a moment before nodding. "Fair enough, my lady. The same as an employee must expect from his employer."

Udora's gaze flicked away from his for an instant, then returned to match stare for stare. After all, hers was but a mild deception. What were two more husbands added to the list when one had already revealed a previous two? His own reticence to expose his true identity was far more reprehensible than her paltry attempt to dissemble.

She smiled up at him. "Suffice to say that a nod from me and you would no longer be in my employ."

His hands tightened on her shoulders. He returned her smile. "A change of heart from me, my lady, and you would no longer benefit from my services." One look at the distraught expression on her face and his smile widened into a grin. "It appears that we have reached a stalemate."

"So it seems, Mr. Bently."

"Then I assume you have no plan to discharge me?"

"Not if you continue to follow my orders."

"To restate my loyalty, Lady Udora. Your wish is my command."

"As it should be."

He should have been forewarned by the smug look on her face, but too late, Bently realized he had fallen into her trap. She placed her hands on his forearms and fixed him with her gaze.

"And speaking of loyalty," she continued as if there had been no lapse of time, "it is my wish that you stand as my escort at our house party next week."

He ran his hand across his chin. "Surely you jest. I could hardly be considered an appropriate escort taking into fact my, uh, my indisposition."

"Are you suggesting that your slight infirmity might suffice to excuse you, or is it your lowborn position to which you refer?"

His face stiffened and he released her to step back. It was a moment or two before he turned to meet her gaze, his hands knotted behind him. He sketched the semblance of a bow. "If truth be told, my lady, either one would be reason enough for you to find a more suitable prospect."

"Suffice to say, there is no one I would rather have standing at my side, Mr. Bently."

He looked extraordinarily pleased, but at the same time Udora detected a wily look in the twinkle of his eyes. He came closer and reached for her hands. "I am most honoured, my lady, but have you no fear that your reputation might be compromised?''

She laughed. ''Look around you. We are quite alone. Our boat is sinking. We are without hope of immediate rescue. I would say that whatever reputation I have left will be thoroughly compromised by the time someone thinks to search for us.''

''I blame myself for putting you in this awkward position.''

''We will survive. We need not think on the blame.''

He pulled her against him, his voice husky. ''For the past months, Udora, I have only had one thought worth thinking.''

There was no need to question him further. His actions provided all the answers. When her arms went around him he cupped her face in his hands and kissed her long and deeply. For the first time in her life, Udora forgot about her previous lovers. She was transported to unexpected heights of rapture that both surprised and delighted her. Holding her here in his arms was the dark-caped horseman she had first glimpsed riding down out of the hills to challenge her. Here at last was a man who could master her will as no other man, be he husband or lover, had ever been able to do.

She felt herself surrender to him. Alas, she mused, not surrender, for every fibre of her being pulled him to her and her to him in a mutual blending of desire. Joined as they were in a passionate kiss, she wished it could last forever, but he was the first to pull away.

His voice rasped in his throat as he held her at arm's length. ''Udora, we must stop or I promise you, I will not be responsible for my actions.''

She brushed her mouth across his, once then twice. "I would not hold you responsible, Aaron, no more than I blame the sun for hiding its light behind the hills at night."

He smiled. "But I would never forgive *myself* if I yielded now to temptation."

She leaned back in his arms. "Then you admit that I tempt you?"

He groaned. "It would be far wiser to admit nothing, given my present condition, and under the present circumstances, but I find it impossible to deceive you."

His words struck a warning chord and Udora stiffened, then pulled away. "Indeed, Aaron Bently, Earl of Kesterson. For one incapable of deception, you have been remarkably successful."

He blanched. "So you know. My dear, I've been wanting to tell you for some time but the appropriate moment never occurred. When did you find out?"

She fluttered her hands. "Oh... long ago. Almost from the very first."

"Indeed?" His voice held no humour. "If that is true, then I grant you your talents as a guardian are sadly wasted. You should be on the stage."

She bristled. "Are you questioning my veracity?"

"Certainly not, my lady. No more than I would question the number of times you have traipsed down the marriage lane."

She gasped. "I... who told you? It was Maggie, wasn't it? Or Taz."

"Just how many times have you been married? I know about two of them, but there was another, was there not?"

Udora hesitated. "Uh, yes. There was another."

He lifted his gaze to the sky. "Then I was right. You were dissembling when you spoke of two marriages?"

"I was not being untruthful. You simply asked if I had been married more than once. When you assumed it was twice, I merely permitted you to draw your own conclusions."

"Yes, I suppose it could have happened that way," he said, stroking his chin. "A sin of omission." He looked up sharply. "But I warrant it won't happen again. Just how many times were you married, Udora? Three, four, ten?"

She averted her face. "Four."

"God's teeth!" He strode across the shale, leaned his hand against a tree and then returned to face her. "So it's four, now. Is that all? Tell me, Udora. Are any of them still in existence?"

"No, Aaron. They're all gone. I've been widowed four times over."

"Why didn't you tell me?"

"I—I really don't know. I was afraid it might distress you."

"It might have if any one of them had been poisoned or reached his demise in some other inopportune way," he said drily, "but I quote the gossips when I say 'that they all appeared to have died with smiles on their faces.'"

She looked up sharply. "Gossip? Then you knew about this all along?"

"Almost from the beginning," he said, mimicking her words.

"Aaron Bently, you are insufferable."

"And you are bewitching, Udora Middlesworth...or whatever your most recent name might be."

She resisted his embrace until she looked at him. His eyes bespoke a need so great that she shuddered and reached out to him with both hands. "It seems, Aaron, that we both are guilty of dissembling."

"Never again, Udora. From now on there's nothing but truth between us."

She felt the thudding of his heart beating against her breast, and she chuckled as she thought how wrong he was. If she had her way, and there was no reason to believe she wouldn't, there would be a *lifetime* between them. But first she must reassure herself that the passion they shared could turn to love.

From all accounts it was well into the afternoon before anyone took their absence seriously. It was not until Mrs. Kragen sent a messenger to Partridge Run that they learned that both Udora and Lord Kesterson were missing. A search party was organized, but they turned up nothing until the following morning when a tenant farmer's son was sent in a boat to search the island. The two of them were discovered huddled together in the comparative comfort of a duck-hunting box. Apparently their horse and gig had not been located till morning, causing a further delay in their rescue.

In no time the boy rowed them back to shore, where they were met by a gaggle of well-wishers running towards them. Udora whispered to Aaron, "Would it not be wise to caution the boy to keep silent about precisely where he found us?"

"Would it serve the purpose?"

Udora sighed. "I suppose not. The youth will spread the word regardless of how we threatened or rewarded him."

"Indeed. You know of course that we're in for a wigging."

She mused. "I suppose I could say that I became ill and you couldn't risk moving me."

He snorted. "If you could see the sparkle in your eyes and the glow on your cheeks you would know how foolish your suggestion is. Perhaps this time you will accept my offer of marriage. You know it is the only way to preserve your reputation."

"But we are guilty of nothing, Aaron, save perhaps a passing thought to temptation," she added with a mischievous smile. "You are most generous, but I have never accepted a proposal simply to save my reputation."

He had no opportunity to protest that he loved her, because Udora gathered her cloak around her. "Ready, Aaron? Here they come. 'Tis far too late to escape our fate."

The girls were the first to arrive. Amy, with her tear-stained face, Em, looking owl eyed and worried, Taz...ah yes, Taz, Udora thought. Taz with the knowing look in her eyes. She missed nothing. There were hugs all around and cheers and smiles from the assembleed servants from both houses.

Maggie took Udora aside and wrapped her in a warm cloak. "An' 'ow was 'e, m'lady?" she asked slyly.

"Don't be a fool, Maggie," Udora sputtered. "We were marooned for a few hours. That doesn't mean we were lost to our proprieties."

Maggie grinned. "Right you be, but there's to be the divil to pay. I 'opes 'imself was worth it."

"Oh, for... Pistachions! For once I suppose I'll learn how it feels to be fodder for the gabble-grinders when I've done nothing that could possibly deserve it."

"Yes, ma'am." Maggie helped her into the gig. "Mrs. McMasters says to tell you she has hot food waiting for you and Mr. Bently."

"Mr. Bently is going home to Partridge Run."

"Aye, but 'e'll be back, I warrant, sooner 'an the coffee leaves the pot."

Udora laughed. "You are incorrigible, Maggie, but yes indeed, I rather think he will."

Word of Udora and Bently's misadventure spread through Coventry before a cat can lick it's ear. The gossip mongers gnawed each piece of news to the bone, despite the fact that the constable discovered that the boat had been deliberately sabotaged. Dodson was the most likely culprit, but as soon as the news of their rescue began to circulate, Dodson was known to have purchased a ticket on a mail coach leaving for London. Since that morning no one had seen hide nor hair of his scrawny body, a fact which left Udora somewhat comforted.

The gossip had one interesting effect. The idea of a country house party so close to the opening of the London Season, had suddenly become all the kick. Those top-lofty matrons who had so easily declined, begging previous engagements, now discovered their calendars to be quite empty on that particular night. Knowing she had the upper hand, Udora took her sweet time in sending a second invitation.

In truth, her time was quite taken up with a million and one obligations. There was the dressmaker to be supervised as well as the gardeners, the drapers and the bevy of local help to be instructed in duties unfamiliar to them.

Mrs. McMasters was only too willing to share the housekeeping duties with a young servant she had tutored while working at The Lark's Nest during the months when Udora and Yvette had held their scandalous Thursday-night soirees. Smoked ducks and pheasants now hung in neat rows in the cold room belowstairs along with baskets of fruits and vegetables and jars of sweetmeats waiting on shelves for the three days of festivities to begin.

Yvette Waverly, Lady Bancroft, whom Udora considered her best friend and confidant, sent her own personal French pastry chef to Coventry to help prepare for the festivities. She herself was unable to attend, having just given birth to her first child, a healthy girl named Annette, after Andrew's maternal grandmother. Andrew, Lord Bancroft, had become the perfect, if somewhat doting father, according to Yvette. He had even forgone his occasional evening at White's club in favour of spending the time with his daughter.

Upon reading her letter, Udora felt a twinge of remorse at having not returned to London for Yvette's lying-in. It was the first time she had not been present when Yvette needed her but it hadn't been possible to leave. So much had changed since those enchanting days at The Lark's Nest.

So much indeed, she mused. She had gone from companion to guardian. A challenge if ever there was one. If truth be told, there were times when she missed the music and dancing and the latest *bon mot* and that indescribable feeling of *vivre le jour* that was so much a part of the London Season.

She held Yvette's letter to her breast. But she needn't be envious any longer. Now there was Aaron. And the party. Life at Amberleigh was certain to be different. She sighed with satisfaction, then turned as Emmy flounced into the room and dropped into a chair.

"I shan't attend the party, after all." She scowled at Udora over the top of her spectacles. "I've made up my mind and that's all there is to it."

Udora laid the letter on the table. "And why have you come to such a formidable decision, if I may enquire?"

"It's Sally."

"Sally? I thought the three of you were getting on quite well with your abigail."

"She says I'm not to wear my spectacles to the ball because they make me look like a bluestocking."

Udora considered the wire-rimmed glasses which magnified Emerald's blue-green eyes. "A bit of an exaggeration, to be sure, but the girl does make a point. And she's no blockhead. Sally trained with the best at the London house of Lady Cowper."

"But if I do not wear them, then pray tell me how am I to see?"

"Well we shall have to think on it. Whilst I do that, you may go to the sewing room and see how your dress is coming along."

"It's almost finished. Miss Colton is just adding another row of lace at the top."

"Indeed? Under whose direction, may I ask?"

"I told her to. There was too much of me showing at the top."

"Emerald, my dear, there is one thing you must learn: that a woman must begin at an early age to learn to attract a husband. Although one must be discreet, showing a bit of shoulder is like putting a silk ribbon on a birthday box. It hints that there is something special inside but doesn't reveal precisely what it is."

Emerald looked owl-eyed. "That's silly. I don't want to attract a husband. Boys are silly...and...and chuckleheaded."

"I'm sure I must have felt that way at your age."

"Did you really?"

Udora thought for a moment. "No, now that I consider, I don't believe I ever did. Fact of the matter is, I was chasing our stableboy into the barn before I reached age ten, but don't let me hear you telling this to Taz or I'll ring a peal over you. She's already too puffed up in her own consequence."

Udora reached for Emerald's hand and held it in hers. "Dear child, the love of books is the most wonderful gift our fathers could have given us. But the time will come when you will meet a man who turns your blood to liquid gold just with the light of his smile. When that happens, my darling, I want you to be ready for him. Do you understand?"

Em nodded. "Yes, my lady."

"Good. Then what we shall do, I think, is to order the most beautiful pair of spectacles we can find, and have them delivered here in time for the ball. Does that please you?"

Em nodded, tears in her eyes. They were both surprised when their arms met in a warm embrace.

CHAPTER NINE

THE FIRST GUESTS began to arrive at midday on Friday. It was with some difficulty that Udora managed to assemble her small brood to greet them. Amy, shy as always, hung back until Emmy could be pried free from a book she was reading. And Taz...Udora sighed. Taz was finally discovered playing with the four cats in the stable hayloft. It took a major effort on the part of Sally and Maggie combined to brush the burrs from her hair and get her into an acceptable gown to receive company.

Udora gave her nod of approval as the girls stood waiting, Amy in soft pink with violet ribbons, Emmy in moss green and Topaz in pale yellow. The cats had followed her into the house, Prometheus, as usual, vying for her attention. Udora felt a sudden pang of remorse. There was a time when it was she whom Prometheus would have come to. Now there was never time to enjoy the cats as she had in London. Taz bent to scratch Prometheus behind the ears. Udora's gaze moved from the cat to the three girls, so bright and appealing in their new gowns. Ah, yes, hers was a small sacrifice indeed, considering what she received in return.

The Dewhursts from Hampshire with their two boys were the first to arrive. Udora was pleasantly surprised to see that the boys, becoming young men now, were well turned out and reasonably well looking.

While the family was getting settled into their rooms the girls, gathered downstairs in the library, began to giggle. Emmy pushed her spectacles back up her nose. "Did you hear the way young Lawrence whistles when he breathes? He sounds like a goose in a henhouse."

Taz screwed her face into a surprisingly good imitation of their guest. "His mother walks like a pouter pigeon," she said, stuffing her hands into her bodice and leaning forward so that her derrière thrust upwards and back. The twins tittered and Taz looked properly rewarded.

"Now, girls," Udora said, trying to hide a smile. "We must remember that these people are our guests and we are to treat them with respect. I'm sure they could find much about us that they would consider laughable."

Emmy pulled her glasses down to the end of her nose and crossed her eyes in a most unbecoming fashion. "I cawn't imagine what it would be," she said, in an affected voice.

Even Udora found it impossible not to laugh, more at Emmy's uncharacteristic attempt at levity than the outlandish expression on her sweet face. Udora clapped her hands. "Enough of this nonsense. Never forget that we are ladies. I admit that the Dewhurst heirs are not what I have in mind as an alliance for any one of you girls, but they will make suitable partners on which to practice your social skills."

Taz settled a steady gaze on Udora's face. "Just who *did* you have in mind for us, Lady Udora?"

"Well, I—" she began, but Amy clasped her hands together and interrupted in an enraptured voice.

"I want a boy with golden hair and eyes so clear and blue that they look like the sky on an April morning."

Taz snorted. "And I suppose Em wants a boy who can read a book a day and speaks seven languages."

They all turned to Em. She frowned and replaced a leather bound copy of *Eastwick's Botany* on the shelf. "I rather think three languages are adequate. Besides, once you've acquired the knack, it's not at all difficult to learn another language or two."

Udora smiled. "Very good. And what about you, Taz. What kind of boy appeals to you?"

Taz looked taken aback for an instant, but she recovered quickly and tossed her silvery-blond hair over her shoulder. "When I choose, he will be a man, not a boy. I want someone, a ship's captain, perhaps, who can fly with the wind." The moment she said it she looked stricken. It wasn't like Taz to reveal so much of herself. Before anyone could say anything, she spun around and left the room.

Udora shook her head. "Pity the poor man. She'll lead him a merry chase." But she smiled when she said it because this was the first time that Taz had ever hinted that she was even remotely interested in finding a husband.

BEFORE THE EVENING CLOSED into night, Amberleigh was filled with visitors from as far away as Cornwall. Among the notable were the Duke and Duchess of Heatherfield. Udora hoped to curry their favour, knowing that their son, William, would be next to inherit. At seventeen he had already been given two of his father's lesser titles.

The bailiff's cottage and stable, now cleaned and refurbished, housed drivers and grooms of those guests who would stay overnight. Keeping a leisurely schedule, as was typical of country house parties, the guests were free to entertain themselves as they might. The gentlemen were drawn to games of battledore and shuttlecock while the women worked at their stitchery or strolled the gardens, keeping watchful eyes on their sons and daughters who indulged in mild flirtations during walks on the promenade and singing games played on the grass.

As promised, Aaron spent the evening at Amberleigh as unofficial host. Following an early supper when the ladies retired to the drawing-room to leave the gentlemen to their port, it was Aaron whom the men addressed. Although Udora's pleased expression left little doubt that he looked the part of congenial host, Aaron was less than comfortable. Not that he lacked social skills; he was as at ease in Carlton House as he was in a Coventry pub. It was his leg. The devilish limp was better now that he was taking the baths at Leamington, but it still nagged him when he stood too long.

Somehow it bothered him less when Udora was close at hand. She was breathtakingly beautiful tonight in her gown of the pure blue of a newly laid robin's egg. Her hair, like spun copper, curled around her face and lay in a glossy coil across one shoulder. He longed to wind it over his fingers and inhale its clean fragrance as he had the night they were stranded on the island. Seeing her tonight so alive and excited was both a joy and a sorrow. Festivity agreed with her; she thrived on it. He had told her that night that she was like a peacock trapped in a chicken coop. How different they were. For despite his title, he was most comfortable playing the role of country squire. And therein lay the rub, for Udora would not long be content without the pomp and circumstance of the London Season.

It seemed to him like hours later when they rejoined the ladies, though a quick look at his fob watch assured him only thirty minutes had elapsed. Udora was involved in an intimate discussion with the dowager duchess when they entered the room. Moments later they separated, and Udora came towards him. She held out her hands and he took them, smiling broadly.

"My dear Udora. You look like the fox who's outsmarted the hounds. What, may I ask, has brought such a gleam to your eyes?"

She dimpled. "Indeed. Am I so transparent? The truth of the matter is that I've just been showing the dowager duchess the Thackery family's collection of porcelain eggs. She was so impressed that she's invited me to bring the girls to take tea at her London house when we go to Town for the Little Season."

"And I presume there is an heir whom you consider possible marriage material?"

"Not in this case, unfortunately. Her grandson, Edgar, is already betrothed to that henwitted little Emerson debutante, though I daresay that is only a minor obstacle. Her grace does, however, have connections with Lady Castlereagh and will put in a word for the girls' bid to Almack's."

"But I thought that you were already on good terms with Lady Castlereagh."

Udora looked appalled. "I am, of course, but one cannot afford to take chances when it comes to Almack's. If any one of the girls was refused a bid, it would destroy us. It would be a disaster. I'd never find suitable matches for them."

"Take my word for it, Udora. The men will flock to them like lambs in new clover."

"Judging by the way Mellingwood has been ogling Topaz, perhaps you're right." She tapped her fan to her chin. "He's a bit into his dotage but come to think on it, there's a potential title there... assuming his brother fails to recover from the gout. And he had good teeth. Surprisingly good for a man his age, don't you agree?"

Aaron grinned. "To be sure. They're Waterloo teeth."

"You don't say!"

"I swear it. My cook heard it from the housekeeper at Devonshire House who heard it from Mellingwood's manservant. It cost a small fortune, too, for teeth yanked from some poor devil who met his maker on the battlefield."

"How unbelievably disgusting." She looked thoughtful. "I wonder, did Mellingwood lose his teeth of natural causes or were they knocked out? We certainly wouldn't want to encourage an alliance with a family whose bones were soft."

Aaron laughed at the outrageousness of her remark. When he saw that she was serious, he managed to control himself, but too late.

She jabbed him with her elbow. "Really, Aaron. If you refuse to take this seriously, then I must move on to more congenial company."

He took her hand in his and held it against his chest. "Come now, Udora. You must admit there is a silly side to this marriage business."

She apparently saw that they were being watched because her face flamed and she tried discreetly to pull away. "Do unhand me, Aaron. Haven't we caused enough gossip with that wretched boating incident?"

"Not quite. But I think this will do it."

He bent and kissed her on the forehead. Udora's gasp was echoed round the room. She forced a smile but spoke through gritted teeth. "You did that deliberately, Aaron Bently. I'll have my revenge for this."

He bowed. "I'm counting on it, my lady." He stepped back and signalled the harpist to retire to the drawing-room for the evening's concert. Udora appeared quite vexed, but there was a gleam in her eyes which had more to do with anticipation than anger. He prayed that he would satisfy her.

A light supper was served just before midnight to accommodate late arriavals. Aaron had been summoned to Partridge Run to supervise the birthing of a foal. Without him, Udora thought, the party had lost much of its glitter. She was grateful when the last guest was sent off to his room and she was able to retire to her own suite. Maggie, looking warm and satisfied as if she had just come from a late romp, was waiting to comb out Udora's hair and hang her gown.

She held the blue velvet out in front of her. "There now, you've gone and ripped it again. 'Tis the third time I've mended the same seam. It's too small for you, I say."

"Nonsense. It fits perfectly. The fault lies with your needlework. Besides, you know very well you're just waiting to get your own hands on this gown."

Maggie thrust out her bosom and slid a hand down the length of her hip. "It would look right foin on me, don't you think?"

Udora threw her hands up in surrender. "Very well. Take it—it's yours. I'm too tired to wrangle."

"Yes, m'lady!" Maggie said as she whisked the gown through the doorway to her own room quicker than a cat licks cream from his whiskers. When she came back to lay out Udora's night rail, she softly closed the door of the armoire. "Word belowstairs is that everyone says the food is the best of any house so far this year."

Udora beamed. "Truly? And the younger members, have you heard anything they may have spoken about the girls?"

"I 'eard one or two snippets. The Wilkersby heir, him being the eldest whose name I don't recall, says Miss Amy is top o' the trees with 'im."

"Hmm. Interesting. There's a certain title there. Of course it could take years."

"Miss Topaz could have old Mellingwood if she wasn't so choicy. He was flashin' them Waterloo teeth o' his at her all night."

"You know about his teeth?"

Maggie gave her a telling look. "Is there anyone who don't?" She grinned. "White as they are they must ha' been plucked from some young buck before 'e was even—"

"Hush. Do let's talk about something pleasant."

Maggie met Udora's reflection in the mirror and batted her eyelashes suggestively. "That bein' Mr. Bently?"

"Really, Maggie. One would think he and I were a *fait accompli.*"

"But the gossips do. Leastwise since you compromised yourself wi' 'im that night on the island."

"And I suppose it will compound the problem at the ball tomorrow night when we lead the dancers onto the floor. But we are perfectly innocent, you know."

Maggie laughed. "Not for me to say, my lady."

"Indeed it is not!"

"O' course there was the other time or two."

"I beg your pardon?" Udora said, looking up sharply.

Maggie waved her hands airly. "Oh, nothing. Just the time you and him was seen kissin' and such." She pulled an innocent face. "O' course it could ha' been that you had a mote in your eye and 'e was just lookin' for it."

Udora stood abruptly. "Enough! I'll finish my toilette myself. Go to bed, Maggie, before I lose my patience."

Maggie chuckled and waltzed towards the doorway. "Good night, m'lady." She turned at the last minute. "I'll knock twice on your door ta wake you in the mornin'. Seein' as 'ow you might not be alone."

She ducked in time to avoid the hairbrush Udora threw at her retreating back.

THE NEXT MORNING began with rain, an ominous sign for any house party, but Udora was confident. She assured her guests as they ambled in for a hearty breakfast at ten, that the rain would cease by eleven, as indeed it did. They entertained themselves with games of whist or hazzard until the sun burned away the dampness and they adjourned to the lawn for amateur theatrics. The younger children were taken in tow by three girls from the village who taught them to play Fox in the Henhouse and other games while their older brothers and sisters played at the game of flirting under the watchful eyes of Maggie and Sally.

Upon being told they were to be chaperoned, Taz had commented with some accuracy that Maggie and Sally were hardly the finest examples of propriety since she had twice seen them wrestling in the hayloft with two farm lads. But it was the best Udora could provide without going to the extreme of hiring the vicar's wife, who was famous for her sour disposition.

Although Udora was beseiged with duties, she still had time to think of Aaron and look forward to the evening when he would arrive to stand with her in the receiving line at the ball. They had yet to dance together. It was something she had anticipated from the moment she had conceived the house party and ball. She was persuaded they would dance together in perfect harmony and look the perfect pair, which could only lead to the perfect proposal. Though he had yet to offer for her, she knew it was just a question of time until he would. There was no doubt in her mind.

But she was taking no chances. The gown she chose for the ball had been selected with unprecedented care. Maggie very nearly swooned when she slipped the ivory brocade over Udora's head.

"Lord 'o mercy, if you don't look like a queen. Are them real pearls?" she asked, referring to the bead-encrusted bodice.

"Only those at the yoke and across the shoulders. The others are costly imitations." Udora powdered her neck and shoulders where the gown cut low both in front and back. Maggie was having trouble with the buttons.

"Do hurry," Udora said.

Maggie smothered an oath. "If 'twas any tighter you'd be burstin' at the seams."

"Don't be absurd. I want the gown to fit well."

"Mr. Bently's sure to think it fits real nice," she said, with exaggerated coyness. "I never did much care for them flat-chested styles them Frenchies wear. You look like a plum ripe for the picking."

"Why, thank you, Maggie. Assuming you meant that as a compliment. I'm sure much of the credit goes to you for the wonders you've worked with my hair."

"Aye. Them pins should 'old it, providin' you stay out 'o the bushes and keeps your dress on."

Udora laughed. "Your impertinence is unbelievable. But just remember, Maggie, it's the girls whom you and Sally are supposed to be watching, not me."

The music was already drifting through the corridors of Amberleigh when Udora gave the nod to Aaron and they led the way towards the ballroom. Needless to say, many of the women had saved their more costly attire for the opening of the London Season a few weeks hence. Even so, the colourful gowns and flash of jewels created an aura of excitement which touched everyone.

Udora was acutely aware that both she and Aaron were being carefully scrutinized by the women. That they were a perfect complement to each other was substantiated by the envious glances sent their way by both men and women. Udora was in transports. It had been a long time, such a very long time, since she had been truly in love.

The girls, along with their contemporaries, who were too young to join in the adult dancing, held their own party in the playrooms. Marcus Andulay, the dancemaster, was present to instruct them in the latest dance fashions. Udora insisted they be taught the waltz, knowing full well that some of the boys' mothers would be furious. It was, after all, considered quite fast. One way or another, she was determined to keep the Thackery name in circulation until the girls could make their bows before the Regent.

Aaron looked strained as he led Udora through the entrance to the ballroom. She tightened her fingers on his arm.

"Do relax, Aaron. The party is a remarkable success. The potted trees were a wonderful idea."

"It's not the cursed trees which concern me, Udora. I warned you, I have no intention of setting foot on the dance floor."

"Of course you will. It isn't as if I'm asking you to dance all night."

"I am not ready to make a bloody fool of myself or you, for that matter, by stumbling about the floor with this damned leg of mine."

Udora forced a smile and a nod as the guests passed through the doorway and began to mill around the edges of the dance floor. She tucked her hand through

Bently's elbow. "Don't be unreasonable, Aaron. You are far too sensitive about your little infirmity." She gazed up at him. "Just one short dance?"

"There are a dozen men who would give their right arm to dance with you." The moment he said it he knew he had said the wrong thing. But the words were out and he couldn't call them back.

Her face froze. "Very well. If that is what you wish, so be it. I bid you good-night, your lordship." She dropped an exaggerated curtsy, then whirled about and marched across the room. All eyes were upon her as she curtsied to Gadsworth, the gaunt and rheumy-eyed Earl of Warminster, then spoke so that everyone could hear. "My lord, would you do me the honour of sharing the first dance?"

"By Gad! Do you mean it?"

"Indeed I do," she said, taking his arm. She nodded to the musicians to begin to play, and the earl, with surprising agility, swept her into the centre of the floor. Udora was determined not to look at Aaron, but a movement caught her eye and she turned her head just in time to see him push his way through the crowd and out the door.

She smothered a colourful oath. She was at fault for her lack of sensibilities. She had, after all, invited him to leave and he had merely taken her at her word. The devil take the man! Any other time he would have stood his ground, told her to accept him as he was. At least she would not have been left looking the fool.

She missed a step in the intricate pattern of the dance, but Gadsworth was far too enthralled to take note. Udora had nodded to the others to join in the dance, a fact which allowed her thoughts more freedom to roam.

If there were only herself to think about she would have gone after Aaron, but this was a Thackery ball and she was the hostess. First impressions were everything. If she chased after him the gossips would cast unflattering allusions not only on her but the girls as well. In the end, she remained behind to charm the guests, but her heart was with Aaron wherever he had gone.

Nor did he return. Long after the party was over and Udora had retired to the vast emptiness of her lonely bed, she continued to dwell on their heated exchange. If only she could talk to him. Never once had they discussed his injury, save to mention that it came as a result of a wound he had suffered during the time he served in France. His lameness was such an intrinsic part of him and he managed so well that Udora rarely gave it a thought.

Before the sun had set the following day, Udora was feeling less charitable. Aaron not only failed to apologize for his unseemly behaviour, he failed to make an appearance as the house guests departed for their homes. After the last carriage had left, the house was disturbingly silent despite the animated conversations of the girls. They, at least, seemed to have enjoyed the festivities, a fact for which Udora was grateful. Nevertheless, she was relieved when they retired for the night. Their frivolous gossip only added to her dismals.

At last alone in her bed, Udora stared at the sliver of moon shining above the amber dome. How long could his silence continue? She was desperate to talk to him, to apologize, if need be. Her resolve strengthened. She needed to speak to him...tonight...before their wounds had time to fester. If only she could find some logical reason to approach him. Of course, there were the accounts. She could question the way he was handling them. No. He would know that for a ruse in an instant. He always kept her informed of everything he did, right down to the last penny.

If this were any other man she had known, husbands included, she would simply appear on his doorstep, no matter how late the hour, and demand an audience. Charles, for instance. Alas, she thought with chagrin, it had been weeks since the dear boy had even crossed her mind. How easy her relationship with Charles had been! To be honest, it was easy because she knew that losing him would be only a minor inconvenience.

But Aaron was different. He wasn't just a man to open doors for her, to squire her to routs and parties and to warm her bed, should she decide to marry him. He had become her world. She could not bear the thought of losing him.

The sound of a howling cat made her sit up straight. Of course! The idea came to her like an answer to a prayer.

Like a flash she was out of bed and flinging open the door to Maggie's room. "Get up, girl. Get up at once."

Maggie gripped the quilt to her chest. "If it ain't the 'ouse afire I ain't stirrin' from me bed."

Udora stripped the blanket to the floor. "Get up and get dressed. Put on something warm, then go to the stable and tell the head groom I want a gig harnessed at once."

"Blimey! Where we goin' this time o' night?"

"Just do as you're told."

Maggie yawned with considerable gusto, then apparently noticed that Udora was still clad in her pistache lace-and-linen night shift. She raised an eyebrow. "So that's it, is it? No need to waste your time puttin' on clothes, then. I'll tell 'im you want the gig promptlike."

"Do that."

Maggie struggled into her clothes and pulled a woollen cloak from her closet. Udora dimly remembered it as one of her own that Maggie said had been left back in London. Well, no matter. Not now, at any rate. She closed the door softly behind Maggie and went to her room to change into something less revealing. The lamplight cast a muted reflection of her in the cheval glass which stood in the corner of the room and she caught her breath. How youthful she looked in this light, her hair cascading about her shoulders in a fiery red glow, her bosom peeking through the pale green lace. Never had she looked so innocent and desirable . . . or felt such an urgency.

Maggie had a point. It would be a shame to waste such an effect. Ah, but decency must prevail. Now, of all times, she must proceed with caution. She selected a woollen gown, cursing the tiny buttons that evaded her trembling hands. A pair of jade-green velvet, fur-lined half boots and a matching full-length Hungarian wrap lined in ivory silk completed her costume. By the time she had brushed her hair and fastened the hood loosely about it, she heard the horse and gig draw up to the front entrance. Maggie had apparently prevailed upon Luther to accompany them. Leave it to the girl to take advantage of the least opportunity.

The cat, tired from his midnight prowling, lay sleeping in front of the fireplace, too innocent and trusting to do more than yawn lazily when Udora picked him up and slipped him, still uncomplaining, into her ample sewing bag.

"There's a good lad, Ulysses," she whispered, holding him close. "If things go well there'll be a dish of cream for you when we return home."

CHAPTER TEN

THE USUALLY CALM MARE was skittish for having been disturbed in the middle of the night, a mood akin to Udora's. Luther urged the horse to even greater speed, slowing only as they rounded the curve near Deep Springs Park. The lovely stretch of woods and grassland was even more beautiful flooded with moonlight and soft shadows. The sound of the mare's hooves on the dirt road surprised a dozen or more deer grazing by the stone wall separating Amberleigh from Partridge Run. They listened for a moment, frozen at attention, then disappeared silently to blend with the undergrowth. Even Luther seemed to be struck with the sheer beauty of the scene.

Ulysses mewed his disapproval at being taken out into the cold night. Maggie took her gaze away from Luther long enough to look startled. "Oiy, was that a cat?"

Udora patted the sewing bag. "I'm taking Ulysses to Aaron. I think the poor dear is ill. Just a bit longer now, my love," she said, wrapping her cloak around the bag.

The manor-house at Partridge Run was dark from top to bottom, a fact which deterred Udora only for the beat of a breath. She was about to instruct Luther to turn the mare towards the main entrance when the light in the windows of the aviary caught her eyes. "All the better," she mused aloud. "It seems Aaron is still at work in the aviary."

Coupled with the cold light of the moon, the glow coming from the window provided enough illumination that they were able to hitch and secure the mare.

"The two of you may wait in the gig," Udora said. "I shan't be overlong." Whether Maggie looked askance, Udora didn't care. As it was, she suspected that Maggie was delighted to have an excuse to spend time alone with Luther.

With the sewing bag tucked under her arm she entered the aviary. Her nose twitched at the moist heat and unaccustomed musky smell of caged birds.

The cat, however, apparently found it quite appealing because he tensed suddenly, let out a howl and lunged out of the bag. Pheasant, partridge, grouse, quail, every kind of game bird known to Udora, wakened in a loud chorus of screeches and beating of wings against cages, which brought Aaron scrambling into the room brandishing a blunderbuss.

Upon seeing Udora, he stopped short. "What in the name of God are you doing here in the middle of the night?"

For a moment she was left speechless. All she could do was point to the cat who was engaged in a staring competition with the caged peacock.

"I...uh...it's the cat. There's something wrong with him. He's...he's been howling most of the night. I—I uh thought that you might give him some medicine...or or something." She saw that he still held the blunderbuss. "I am hardly here alone. Maggie and

Luther are waiting in the gig. And do put away that dreadful weapon."

Bently put the gun down next to the door, then picked up a rug and threw it over the cat. Ulysses fought back but Bently's soothing voice quieted him at once.

Bently carried him through the doorway into his office, then looked back over his shoulder at Udora. "Well, are you coming or would you prefer to stand there and continue to frighten my birds?"

"Don't be tiresome," she said, grasping the edges of her wrap and following after him.

"Close the door after you," he commanded as he lifted the cat to the desk in the middle of the room. In spite of the fact that he was still fully clothed, Udora saw that he must have been sleeping, because a cot at the far end of the room give evidence that he had just tumbled from it.

He slipped the cat into a cage then lighted another lamp and turned the wick up high. The cat, in the meantime, was not at all pleased with the indignity of being held prisoner. He let out a howl that on a darker night would have raised the dead.

Udora smiled at the way Ulysses had entered into her game. "There you see, Aaron? Ulysses seems to be quite ill." She moved next to Aaron and pushed back her hood, allowing her hair to fall freely about her shoulders. At the same time she casually loosened her wrap and undid the clasp which held it in place. Aaron seemed blissfully unaware. She cursed silently. Was he being stubborn, disinterested or was he simply engrossed in playing veterinary?

Opening the door of the cage, he lifted the cat gently onto the desk. It took several minutes for him to run his hands over the animal's body, then to peer into his ears. Ulysses, gentled now by Bently's ministrations, purred loudly and even allowed his mouth to be examined.

Bently straightened. "There's nothing wrong with *this* one, save for the fact that he, ah, is perhaps looking for a mate."

Udora coloured in spite of herself. "Oh, dear me. I hadn't thought of that. I, uh, what should I do?"

Bently gave her a wry look. "I rather imagine he can figure that out for himself." He put the cat back into the cage. "As for myself, however, I would be grateful if in the future you refrained from turning him loose in my aviary."

She managed to look contrite. "Yes, of course. I didn't intend..."

"I should hope not! No need to apologise."

Udora moved closer to him, all the while contriving to look demure but knowing that she failed to fool him. "Actually, I fear I do owe you an apology. I couldn't sleep without making amends for my shortness of temper and my extreme lack of consideration last night. I am truly sorry, Aaron. Please forgive me."

Almost immediately she saw him begin to thaw. Perhaps she hadn't failed, after all. He ran his fingers through his hair. "Again, there is no need to apologise. It was simply a misunderstanding. No harm done." He pushed a roll of papers aside and rested his hip on the corner of the desk. "But in all sincerity, Udora, I continue to agonize over our circumstances. I am well aware of the bond which has formed between us and it troubles me that I cannot be the dashing dandy you would like me to be.''

She stroked his arm. ''Please don't misunderstand. It is not my wish to change you. I simply had no idea that you were so sensitive about your injury.''

He covered her hand with his own and drew it to his cheek. ''I am acutely aware of anything, anything at all which affects the two of us. I know you are not blind to my feelings for you, Udora. From the moment I first saw you I've been driven to touch you, to hold you and tell you of the countless ways I want to make love to you.''

A faint gasp escaped her lips, and she came unhesitatingly into the circle of his arms. He stood and pulled her close to him, entwining his hands in her hair and cupping her head so that his mouth met hers in an achingly sweet kiss. It seemed to last forever, but not long enough to satisfy the yearning that deepened between them with each passing moment.

Seeing the cot in the corner, Udora leaned back to catch her breath. ''I fear we are treading in deep water, Aaron. Perhaps we should return to shore.''

He laughed. ''I won't let you drown, my dearest. Marry me and I'll teach you to swim.''

''Marry you?''

''Don't look so surprised. You must have known I've been contemplating offering for you for some time.''

''No. If truth be told, I didn't know. It was my fervent hope that you cared enough to propose marriage,'' she added with a smile, ''but I thought it would take some strategic manoeuvrings on my part to convince you to speak up.''

"It was my plan to allow you to do so, if only to see what extremes you might be driven to." He pressed a kiss to her forehead. "But I find you too bewitching to resist. What is your answer, Udora? Will you consent to be my wife?"

She lifted her face to his. "Protocol dictates that I refrain from answering without first taking time to think your offer through." She traced her fingers over the strong line of his jaw and across his lips. "Well, I've thought about it long enough, and the answer is yes."

His pleased expression was reward enough for her, but when he kissed her to seal their troth, Udora was euphoric. Several minutes passed before they could bring themselves to move apart. Even then it was doubtful that they could have refrained from touching had not Udora's arm knocked a roll of papers to the floor. She bent to pick it up.

Her attention was caught by the artistic rendering of a map. "Is this something important? How careless of me. I hope I haven't damaged the drawing," she said. "I must have stepped on it."

"It's as nothing. Put it back on the desk, for we have something much more important to occupy ourselves with."

Curiosity prevailed and she unrolled the papers and spread them on the desk. "Why, it's a map of Amberleigh and Partridge Run where they adjoin at Deep Springs Park." She bent closer. "What is this?"

"It's nothing, Udora. Just a bit of scratching."

"Scratching, indeed! The map has been redrawn so that the Park, the piece of land you say I'm to inherit when the girls marry, now lies within the boundary of Partridge Run."

Even in the pale light of the lamp Udora could see the dark flush stain his neck and face. The only sound in the room was the crisp snap of the map when she released her hold on it. She wrapped her arms around her in an unconscious gesture of protection. "What does this mean, Aaron? I demand an answer."

He slowly expelled his breath as he came round the corner of the desk to face her. "It means nothing, Udora. Oh it's true, in the past I've made no secret of the fact that I want very much to own Deep Springs Park. It was once a part of Partridge Run, you know, until my grandfather lost it to the Thackerys. Deep Springs Park and the oak grove at Partridge Run were part and parcel of a grant given to my great grandfather from the Duke of Edinburgh." He ran his hands across his face. "But the fact that you will inherit the land has nothing to do with the way I feel about you."

"Indeed." Her voice, even to her own ears, was as dry as tinder. And like tinder, her happiness went up in smoke. He had been manipulating her from the beginning. All the while he was courting her, he had one purpose in mind: to gain control of Deep Springs Park. Well, he would never succeed. Not as long as she lived.

She turned abruptly, whirling her wrap about her, and swept from the room. Luther and Maggie gaped as she stomped over to the gig. It was only later as she slung open the kitchen door at Amberleigh, that she remembered Ulysses. No doubt Aaron would see to his return. By then, God willing, she would be well on her way to London.

Maggie sought her cot the instant they entered the suite, but Udora had other ideas. "Oh no, my girl. You're going to pack. We're going home."

Maggie gave her a suspicious look. "Was it Mr. Bently what give you such a maggoty notion?"

"Why I have decided to leave is none of your concern. Just do as you're told and waken the girls. Tell them we are leaving for London at first light."

"I'm not goin'. 'Tis a good two weeks 'til the Season starts. We'll all be struck down with Lombard Fever." Maggie attempted to escape to her adjoining room.

"You are to pack this minute, I tell you. And why should you think you'll be struck down with boredom. I thought you couldn't wait to return home."

"Well, things is a mite different now."

Udora huffed. "Now, meaning since you've been meeting Luther in the hayloft over the barn."

Maggie grinned. "An' I can't think of a better reason for stayin' on."

"I seem to remember you called him a country bumpkin."

"A johnny raw 'e might be, but 'e's not one to outrun the constable, which is more'n I can say for Danny Hodges."

Udora flung her valises onto the bed and began to stuff them with clothing. "That is as it may be but you are too young to make a decision. It will do you good to see Danny Hodges when we get home to see if your feelings for him have truly changed."

Sensing that she had no recourse, Maggie dutifully went to waken Sally and the girls. Udora roused the McMasters, who were to accompany them to London. A messenger was sent ahead on horseback to alert the staff who had remained behind at The Lark's Nest to maintain the house. Udora calculated that the notice would provide them with at least a day to ready the house for her arrival.

The sun had only begun to rise in the eastern sky when they took their departure. It had been difficult to leave the cats behind, but should this return to London become more than a temporary respite, she would send someone to fetch them home. In the meantime, Mrs. Kragen would resume her command over the household, and Aaron, gentleman that he was in most things, could be counted upon to continue on as bailiff.

Ah, yes, Aaron. Though it pained her to think about him, she knew she would remember him always with both joy and sorrow, for she had come to love him as she had loved no other man. Even though he had appeared to love her as a means to his own ends.

Udora set her mouth in a grim line. Never again would she allow herself to be hurt in such a way. Had he come after her at once she might have forgiven him, but no. The hurt went too deep for such a small compensation. It was over. She had to get on with her life.

AS THE CARRIAGE RUMBLED along the turnpike, she gazed at the sleeping twins. They had been none too happy about the sudden change in plans. Topaz, on the other hand, was as alert as a cat at a mouse parade.

"Are there horses at The Lark's Nest?"

"Not at present, but we can rent them at Mr. Tilbury's Stables on Mount Street and ride in the Park."

"And is there boating nearby?"

"I'm sure there is, although it's been years since I sailed on the Thames." Udora adjusted her bonnet. "My dear, you should be less concerned with sporting and entertainment and more concerned about finding a suitable young man to squire you about, with the proper supervision, of course."

"Young men are far too boring."

"Pistachions! It is only a question of attracting the right one."

Topaz tossed her bonnet back and allowed her curls to spring forth. "Pistachions, indeed. It is he who should attract me, not the other way round."

Udora laughed aloud not only at Topaz's unbridled confidence, but at the girl's purloining of Udora's own private expletive.

Mrs. McMasters started suddenly from her nap in the corner of the carriage. "Wh—what is it? Is it a highwayman?"

"Nothing so dramatic, my dear. Only an optimistic flight of fancy from our Miss Topaz."

Topaz flashed her a challenging look. "We'll see."

Udora settled back and closed her eyes. Yes. She was acutely aware of the fact that time would tell all. It always did. The dull ache returned to the pit of her stomach. She knew it was not that she had forgotten to eat breakfast. This was simply one more pain she could lay at Aaron's feet.

THE BIERLEYS, the young couple whom Udora had hired to supervise the care of The Lark's Nest while the McMasters were established at Amberleigh, had everything at the ready when Udora's entourage arrived in St. John's Wood. A small staff of temporary hires had aired the house, provided fresh linens, stocked the pantry and tidied the grounds, all in a day's time.

Emerald, Amethyst and Topaz were delighted with the cottage, which seemed to them like a doll's house after the sprawling expanse of Amberleigh. Amy and Taz explored the attic while Em, true to form, planted herself in the library with a stack of books.

Not more than two hours had elapsed when a visitor was announced. Charles! Maggie took one look at Udora and reached for a comb. "You might best tell McMasters you ain't receiving yet. Leastways 'till I have a go at your hair."

"Nonsense. Besides, it's only Charles come to call. There's no need to put on airs with him."

"And no need to burn your bridges, either, him bein' the only swell left on your string and you not gettin' any younger."

"And what do you mean by that?" Udora demanded, settling herself in the chair facing the dressing table.

Maggie sniffed. "Even a sapscull could guess that you and Mr. Bently have broken spokes and gone your separate ways, else why would you have trundled off to London in high dudgeon?" She twisted the copper curls around her finger and pinned them into place before handing Udora the mirror. Maggie laid the comb on the dressing table. "If 'twas me, I'd cut me a dash wi' Mr. Willingsly before 'e took French leave. 'E won't wait forever, you know, 'im and 'is blunt.

'E's not the man to sit long for your birdwitted notions."

"I don't know how I survived for so long without your advice," Udora said dryly. "Now if you will allow me, I have matters to attend to."

"And no doubt make a muddle o' them," Maggie said to herself, knowing that anyone within a stone's throw could hear.

Udora pretended to ignore her. She chewed her lips to bring out the colour before going downstairs to the library where Charles was awaiting her. It would be lovely to see him again. In many ways he had filled the empty spaces in her life with his charm and *savoir vivre*. Was Maggie right? Should she be more prudent than to burn her bridges with the past?

An unfamiliar young footman opened the door for her when she approached the library. One of Mrs. Brierley's new hires, Udora thought. It was only after he closed the door behind her that she realized she had failed to notice whether he was handsome. Maybe Maggie was right. She *was* getting old.

Charles rose and came towards her before she had a chance to greet him.

"Zounds, old girl! You've grown even more beautiful since I last saw you." He took her lightly in his arms and kissed her on the cheek.

Udora returned the embrace with less pleasure than she cared to admit. Compared to Aaron, Charles was such a greenhorn, albeit a handsome one. Even his most fervent embrace paled compared to Aaron's barely leashed passion. She smiled widely, feigning enthusiasm whilst trying to push Aaron firmly from her mind.

"Charles, my pet. You look handsome as always. It's been a long time, hasn't it?"

"Only a few weeks but it seems like an age. London hasn't been the same without you. Thank heaven I returned early from our country house or I wouldn't have known you'd come home."

He held her at arm's lenght. "Are you here to stay? I've spread the word that you're in Town, my dear, so in no time we'll be deluged with invitations."

"I've scarcely had time to remove my travel dirt," Udora protested, at the same time making note of his use of the term *we*.

"Tell me you've come to your senses and left those obnoxious children behind." Before she could respond, he continued. "I have only just been handed the most exciting invitation to spend a few days at Windsor Castle. I want you to come with me, old girl, providing you are not encumbered with that trio of hell-cats."

Udora stiffened. "Mind your tongue, Charles. Those hell-cats, as you choose to refer to them, are very dear to me. Indeed, where their welfare is concerned, I regard them as my very own flesh and blood."

He shook his head in wonderment. "God's teeth! What have they done to you? Udora, old girl, you used to call me stuffy, but you have me beat all to hollow. I think you've become—" his eyes bulged "—domesticated!"

She stepped back. "Strange as it may seem, Charles, you are not entirely wrong. A few weeks ago I would have scoffed at the thought of being a surrogate mother, but now I find that my three girls are the most important thing in the world to me."

"And where does that leave me? I came here to give back the ring you returned to me before I left Amberleigh. Father insisted, and even Mother that I come to terms with your, ah, colourful background. As for me, you know you mean everything to me and it's time we got buckled."

They were interrupted by a knock and the young footman opened the door. "Begging your pardon m'lady, but McMasters says as how the gentleman's horses is raisin' a bit of a breeze."

Charles wiped his hands on his breeches. "Forgive me, Udora. I must attend to them." He looked faintly embarrassed. "They are a blooded pair and, well, I wouldn't want them to come to any harm. We'll talk again."

"Not today, Charles. I fear everything is quite at sixes and sevens and I have no time for callers."

He bowed. "As you say."

Udora sank down in the nearest chair and closed her eyes.

"I think he cares more for his horses than he does for you."

Udora looked up sharply and saw Emerald peering over the back of a Queen Anne chair.

"I might have known you'd be here. My dear child, good manners would dictate that you make yourself known when people enter a room."

Emerald came round the end of a table and seated herself on an ottoman at Udora's feet. "I heard what you said."

"Indeed? And what was that, pray tell?'

Emerald fidgeted with her spectacles. "What you said about us, I mean. It's true, isn't it, like Amy said? You really do care about the three of us."

"I was hoping that I had made my regard for you very clear from the beginning."

"I have regard for our cook and butler but I don't love them."

Udora smiled. "So you're finally willing to admit that I love you and will stay with you always. In truth I was beginning to fear that only your books were worthy of your affection."

A smile flickered across Emmy's face. "Books are friends when you don't have any. But I like you way better." She twisted a curl around her finger. "You've made us feel like a family again."

Udora leaned forward and hugged her. "Then whatever happens to me I will have that knowledge to cherish."

Emmy returned the embrace then folded her hands on her lap. "You were thinking of him just then, weren't you?"

"Him? You mean Charles Willingsly?"

Emmy gave her a speaking look. "I mean Mr. Bently, Lord Kesterson, of course. He's in love with you, you know. He even told me so once when I visited his peacock."

"The truth of the matter, dear child, is that he wants to marry me... but not because he loves me."

"He has buckets of money and more to spare. It can't be for your money."

"No, dear. Not for my money."

"Then what?"

"I know you mean well, Emmy, but I find it very painful to discuss at this time."

Emmy tucked her hands under her knees and leaned forward. "I know! It must be Deep Springs Park? The parcel of land you are to have when the three of us wed?"

Udora tensed. "How did you know? Did he say something to you?"

Emmy looked pained. "Not exactly. I, uh, found a copy of my father's will in a strong box. Naturally I was curious." She shrugged. "And Bently did mention once that my grandfather had swindled his grandfather out of the Deep Springs Park land and Bently wanted to get it back."

"Surely you must be wrong."

Emmy was outraged. "I never say anything I can't prove, Lady Udora. It's all there in my family's private journals."

"Which you have doubtless contrived to read," Udora said, hoping to change the subject.

"I thought it would be all right. They belong to us now. Amy and Taz don't care a fig about them, but I think they are interesting."

"Point made. And since you seem to have taken charge of them, it might well behoove you to continue the entries."

"Do you think it would be all right?"

"I think it's a splendid idea. Perhaps it will improve your writing."

Emerald made a face. "You sound like my tutor. Are we to stay in London, then?"

"For a time, yes. I think it might be good for the three of you to be exposed to Polite Society before your come-out. Does the idea distress you?"

Emmy shrugged. "Not if I am free to peruse the library. I've discovered some splendid tomes on the history of the Elizabethan reign and its effect on foreign policy during her later years."

Udora rolled her eyes to the ceiling. "I see I have my work cut out for me. Well, never mind, Emmy. Do as you wish for now, but very soon we must begin to think about your future."

It occurred to Udora more than once as the days progressed that Aaron Bently had made no attempt to pursue her. Any one of her former beaux would have done so without hesitation. But Aaron was different. He was strong! Disciplined. She supposed it was his military background. Pistachions! Was it *she* who would have to go to him if they were ever to resolve their differences?

Had she the chance to play over her sudden departure from the aviary that night, she would delay at least long enough for him to explain as he said he could.

For always, tormenting her night or day, were Emmy's words.

"He loves you, you know. He even told me so one day."

CHAPTER ELEVEN

SMALL ACHES EITHER disappear entirely or grow into large aches, Udora decided as she arrived in Mayfair to call on Yvette Waverly, Lady Bancroft and her new daughter. It was sadly apparent that the ache in her heart that was Aaron Bently was not going to disappear. Added to the inevitability of carrying the pain was the fact that she was unable to hide her feelings. Particularly from Yvette who, during the two years they spent together at The Lark's Nest, had become her most intimate friend and confidante.

Udora managed to put off the inquisition until after the new baby, Annette Louise, had been held, admired, chucked under the chin and returned to the waiting arms of the wet-nurse.

Udora sighed. "She is such a dear. I do hope you will permit me to bring the girls to see her."

"But of course. And I look forward to seeing the Thackery Jewels," she said, laughing. "What an unbelievable shock it must have been to inherit three nearly grown children instead of a handful of diamonds."

"To call it a shock is like calling the war with France a minor inconvenience, but in truth, Yvette, I have learned a great deal more about myself in the past few weeks." She hadn't meant to sound so somber.

Yvette took one look at her and reached for her hands. "*Chère amie,* what is it about you that has changed? You look so lovely, even more so than when you so hastily took your departure from London so many weeks ago." She shook her cap of blond curls. "*Tiens!* But the eyes. I see so much sorrow there. What has happened to you?"

Udora forced a laugh. "Charles tells me I've become domesticated."

"No! No, this... this sadness I see in your eyes has nothing to do with the children. I think perhaps it is an *affaire de coeur,*" she said, placing her hand over her heart.

Udora sank down onto a chaise longue. "It wasn't my intention to speak of it, but you are far too awake to my feelings for me to hide anything from you."

"Aha, then it is a man. Who is he? *Nom de Dieu!* Don't tell me he is already married."

"No. Nothing like that. He is my bailiff."

"My dear Udora. Surely not!"

Udora gave her a wry look. "I'm surprised the gossips have not spread the word to London by now. We are quite the latest on-dit, particularly since we spent the night alone on a deserted island in the middle of the river."

"Something you secretly arranged, no doubt," Yvette said with a twinkle in her eye.

"Not this time. A few mere months ago, perhaps, but now that I am a surrogate mother, I never permit myself such adventures. Well, almost never," she added, thinking of the night she took the cat to the aviary.

"Then begin at the beginning and tell me everything," Yvette commanded, settling herself on a chair across from Udora.

"Oh, my dear. It seems more like a year than merely a few weeks, but I shall try." Udora talked for nearly an hour when Yvette sent for a tea tray and they dallied for another hour sipping tea and nibbling on brandied fruit tarts.

Later, back at The Lark's Nest, Udora marvelled that she had spoken so freely. A twinge of regret washed over her, but she knew in her heart that sharing her disappointment over Aaron Bently, was the first step towards soothing her pain. That it would never heal was a forgone conclusion. Nor did she want it to. For the bittersweet memories of the time they had spent together were all that she had left of him.

The cottage was uncomfortably quiet until the girls returned from their outing with Maggie and Sally as chaperones. Udora was grateful for their exuberance. "And what did you think of Westminster Abby? Did you see the great Coronation Chair? And the tombs of the kings and queens? And of course you saw the Houses of Parliament as you approached the Abbey."

Amy flung herself into a chair and kicked off her slippers. "And we saw the most wonderful thing. A travelling show with wax figures of famous people. The best one was Cleopatra. She was so beautiful."

"You saw Madame Tussaud's Museum? Really, Maggie, I thought you and Sally would have been more prudent. I want the girls to see and hear things of lasting value."

"It wasn't their fault," Emerald said, scowling over the top of her spectacles. "We saw the posters and decided to go in."

Maggie sniffed. "If 'twas good enough for the duke, 'tis good enough for the likes o' them."

Amy nodded vigorously. "It's true you know. The exhibit is highly recommended by the Duke of Wellington."

"And we saw other posters, too," Topaz said breathlessly. "One of them was of a man in a balloon. He's to be flying again in two weeks at Vauxhall Garden." Her face was flushed with excitement.

Udora gave her a speaking look. "That's all well and good, my dear, but one mustn't become swayed from our purpose. We have come to Town to further your chances of finding successful matches, not simply to be entertained. There is time enough for that once you are offered for." She walked to the window and pushed aside a silken drapery. "To that end I have decided to hire a tutor and a dancemaster to take over where your former teachers left off."

The three girls groaned as one. Udora brushed their protest aside with a wave of her hand. "It will do you no good to fret. This is something that must be done. Once you have come-out there will be time enough for frivolities."

Amy straightened and folded her hands in her lap. "I am quite ready to do as you say, my lady. How soon are we to make our formal bows?"

"I am thinking seriously about the Little Season. It is but a few months away and you will have turned sixteen by then. but there is much to be done before August. The Lark's Nest is too small, of course, for the Grand Ball that must follow your presentation." She tapped her hand to her cheek. "But perhaps Lady Waverly or Lord and Lady Carstairs would allow us the use of their ballroom. Berrington House would be so perfect! And your gowns! They must be unique, the height of fashion. We must search the magazines for drawings that we might have copied by the seamstresses. My dears! We have work to do."

Amy listened with rapt attention, but Udora noticed that Em had already drifted towards the glassed cabinet to search for a book. Seeing that Topaz was busy at her sketchpad, Udora smiled with satisfaction until she saw that the drawing was of a multicoloured balloon floating high about the treetops.

Udora picked up the glossy coil of silvery-white hair which fell over Topaz's shoulder and smoothed it down her back. "My dear child, you have an excellent sense of composition, but you must learn to restrain your fantasies until such time as you have wed or are at least betrothed."

Taz laid the bit of crayon on the table and looked up. "If I do as you say—" she scowled "—and prepare myself to be auctioned off to the highest bidder, will you let me take a ride in the balloon?"

Udora laughed. "At your age I would have bargained for much more. A diamond clip... an ermine wrap, at the very least."

"I thought of asking to *buy* a balloon, but since I don't know how they work as yet, I must also have someone to fly it for me." She looked up from lowered lashes. "Then you agree?"

The intense glitter that Udora saw in Topaz's eyes should have warned Udora but so intent was she on her one and only purpose that the moment passed and she gave her word.

Emmy proved to be a lesser problem. She was amenable to most things as long as one made it a point to keep the interruptions from her reading both brief and of the utmost importance.

All four of the women were at loose ends without the cats to entertain them in their quiet moments. Udora, having been forced to accept the fact that Aaron Bently was disinclined to chase after her, sent a messenger to Amberleigh to retrieve the four felines. Two days later the messenger returned but with three of the cats. Ulysses was missing. Udora was horrified. She grabbed the messenger by his coat lapels and demanded an explanation. The suddenness of the attack frightened him so that he went weak in the knees and had to be offered a chair.

Udora loomed over him. "Well, speak up. What have you done with Ulysses?"

"N-n-nothin', me lady. Sure as God is me witness I didna' tech a hair o' his head. 'Twas the gent who 'ad 'im an wouldna' let 'im go."

"What gentleman? What are you trying to say?"

"'Ere it is," he said, rummaging through his cloak. "A letter wot 'e said I should give you."

Udora didn't need to see the heavily embossed coat of arms to know that the letter was from Aaron Bently. The paper, the colour of rich cream, still bore the faint fragrance of bayberries that she had come to associate with him. She held the letter to her breast and excused herself in order to read in private.

"My Dear Lady Udora," the letter began. A formal enough beginning, Udora thought, her stomach tightening.

> Your messenger arrived at Amberleigh today to remove the cats to London. I understand this as an indication that you do not soon intend to return to Coventry. For this reason I have taken it upon myself to assume possession of one adult male named Ulysses. The male in question has seriously jeopardized the reputation of a female under my protection, namely, one Snowball, a resident at Partridge Run. Thanks to Ulysses's lack of restraint and consideration, Snowball is currently *enciente*, or to put it more bluntly, in the family way, a fact which I find deplorable.

Udora laughed, shaking her head in disbelief. He was teasing, of course. He couldn't be serious. She read more rapidly, looking for the line that would beg her forgiveness for currying her favours to gain control of Deep Springs Park, but instead he continued in the same vein.

> I trust that you will see to it that the aforementioned Ulysses will do the acceptable thing and take responsibility for his unconscionable misbehaviour. To this end I expect to hear from you forthwith.
>
> Yours respectfully,
> Aaron Bently, Lord Kesterson

Udora read the letter three times before confronting her messenger. "This is the most ridiculous bit of nonsense I've ever heard. Tell me, what else did he have to say?"

The messenger, standing bow-legged and twisting his cap in his hands, looked ready to bolt. "N-nothin' much, me lady, 'ceptin' 'e give me a canary to take the letter to ye and sent me down to ask cook for a mug o' stew to warm me gullet."

"Very well, if that's the way of it. I'll give you another sovereign to take a message back to him. You may sleep first of course, and partake of hot food."

She spoke then to the young footman, giving him orders to see to the man's comfort. Then Udora sat down to write to Aaron. It wasn't as easy as she had anticipated. Her mood went from anger at his unmitigated gall, to confusion as to his motives, to laughter over his utterly unbelievable ploy. Out of desperation she sent the following missive.

My Dear Lord Kesterson,

I cannot countenance the ridiculous charges you levy against my ward, Ulysses, whom you at present hold hostage for whatever reason only God is privy to.

Surely you must realize that Snowball, the female in question, is known for her free and easy ways with the opposite sex, and I daresay, is a *habitué* of the stable and even less respectable establishments. I myself have seen her leaving the milk-house early one morning wearing nothing but a fur coat.

Ulysses, on the other hand, is inexperienced in the ways of the flesh, having lived all his life within the confines of my house. If there was some such transgression as the one to which you allude, and this I sincerely doubt, it would behoove you to offer some sort of proof that it was indeed Ulysses who was the instigator.

In the meantime, sir, I insist that you release your hostage and return Ulysses to me at once. Should you fail to do so, I must regretfully turn this matter over to the proper authorities.

Yours respectfully,
Lady Udora Middlesworth

The messenger left the next morning at dawn. He returned two days later, empty handed, save for another bright new sovereign clutched in his beefy hand, and another letter from Aaron.

Udora, having spent a sleepless two days, tore the letter open with undue haste.

"My dear Lady Udora," it read.

I am shocked by your lack of consideration for the delicate situation in which your charge has left my innocent young Snowball. Suffice to say that there is no question as to who is responsible for her fall from grace. There were two witnesses who will vouch for the fact that it was indeed Ulysses who bestowed his attentions upon her.

I admit, dear lady, that Snowball is a bit of an adventuress, but one could hardly say that she is a *fille de joie.* I find the insinuations just short of slanderous. Ulysses, on the other hand, has become a rakehell and libertine since leaving the protection of your house. As his protector, you and no one else must be held responsible.

Your suggestion that the magistrate be called in to settle this matter is an excellent one. Unless you offer some sort of recompense post haste, I will file an injunction within the week to prevent such an incident from happening again.

I suggest we speak in person before I am forced to take such action. To this end, I will expect you to call upon me within the week.

Yours respectfully,
Aaron Bently, Lord Kesterson

She folded the letter and pressed it to her breast. The messenger shuffled his feet back and forth to get her attention, for it was obvious she was lost in transports.

"Beggin' your pardon me lady. Will you be after sendin' me off to Coventry agin?" It was plain he itched to get his hands on another sovereign or two.

She looked at the window towards the garden, bright now with Spring flowers. "No, Rufus. Not this time. I fear I shall have to go to Coventry for myself."

SHE CHANGED HER MIND a dozen times in the next two days. The journey to Coventry was little short of a fool's errand. Indeed, this whole fuss over Snowball's condition was nothing but childish nonsense. Why then was Aaron so adamant that she return to Amberleigh? Why, indeed? Could it be that he just wanted to see her or was this a last desperate attempt to convince her of his devotion in order to regain control of Deep Springs Park?

And why should she do his bidding? Another man would have come to London to bargain with her. Devil take the man for his strong will. She couldn't fight him. Nor could she stay away from him. Just the thought of seeing him filled her emptiness with a sudden warmth that set her blood to boiling.

But she was needed here. It wouldn't do to drag the girls away from their new tutor and the dancemaster she had hired to oversee their training. Then, too, they had appointments with milliners, modistes and feather merchants to put together their new wardrobes. Neither Maggie nor Sally was skilled enough to make selections from the designs and fabrics which were available.

But Lady Carstairs or the countess would be most capable. And she would be seeing them today at Yvette's home where they were to join Udora and the girls for tea. Her heart quickened at the idea. The countess would love supervising their wardrobes. And it would leave Udora free to return to Coventry.

As good fortune prevailed, both ladies were present when Udora arrived at Bancroft Hall with her charges. They were immediately taken with the girls and seemed delighted to take them under their wings. Udora couldn't have asked for more capable women. The countess was titular head of the Harrington House of Fine Fashions whose styles were respected even among the best houses of Paris.

Fortunately the girls were on their best behaviour. Emerald was enthralled by a recent edition of colour plates depicting the castles of Scotland. Taz sat primly, her hands folded on her lap. It was plain to Udora, if no one else, that her thoughts were far away. It was also quite obvious to Udora that this untypical behaviour boded nothing but trouble. She managed to push it from her mind, though, in her delight over Amy's fascination with baby Annette.

"Would you like to hold her, Amy?" Yvette asked.

"Oh, may I please?"

Her eagerness was so painfully clear that everyone laughed.

"I've never held a real baby before, I mean a baby person. Of course I've held a newborn lamb and fed it milk from a dipper." She held the baby close to her and pressed her cheek against the dusting of golden curls. "I—I don't suppose I could feed her."

Yvette smiled. "I'm afraid, dear child, that we must leave that to the wet-nurse for now."

Everyone laughed except Em, whose attention was still held by the prints and excepting Topaz, who gave Amy a disgusted look.

Amy's face turned bright pink. "Of course. I had forgotten."

Yvette's voice was gentle. "Permit me to say, Amy, *ma chérie,* that I look forward to having you visit Annette whenever possible."

The afternoon was so pleasant that it sped by quickly. Nevertheless, Udora was on tenterhooks until it was time to take their departure. Upon returning to The Lark's Nest, Udora was met by Maggie who, in one of her sulks, was packing a small bag for Udora to take to the country.

"What is it now?" Udora demanded.

Maggie shot her a baleful look. "Nothin'."

"Of course it's something. I know that look on your face."

Maggie contrived to look innocent. "It ain't *my* face what worries me, m'lady."

"Indeed? And what is that supposed to mean?"

"Oh . . . nothin'. I wouldn't want to be causin' you to worry."

"Pistachions! My sensibilities never worried you before. Speak up. What is it?"

"Well. . . since you be after draggin' it out o' me. Tis *you* what worries me. You goin' off to Coventry without so much as someone to look after your 'air and gowns." She shook her head and lifted her gaze to the ceiling. "An' it pains me to know what himself will think, seein' you look like some Grubstreet quiz."

Udora laughed in spite of herself. "Your confidence in my ability to dress myself is hardly reassuring. I presume it is your wish to accompany me to Amberleigh?"

"Oh, no, my lady!" Maggie tossed her head. "'Twould be 'ard on me, the coach ride and all, but for you I would be proud to suffer the torment."

"How considerate of you. And I suppose the fact that Luther Jones will be there waiting in the hayloft has nothing to do with your sudden and most remarkable desire to be of service?"

Maggie grinned. "Aye, you could suppose that."

"I've told you before, my girl, that Luther is not to be trusted. He has a reputation in the village for dancing to the tune but refusing to pay the piper."

"'Tis 'im what pipes the tune for me, m'lady, 'im an them sheep's eyes wot makes the country girls' knees turn to noodles." She fluffed her hair in an effort to characterize a London debutante. "'Tis me what dances," she continued. "Leastwise 'til I thinks o' somethin' more rewardin' to pass the time o' day."

"You watch your step, girl, or you'll be riding back to London in the family way, with no family to speak of."

Maggie's eyes lit up. "Does that mean I'm to go?"

"I suppose it does. But you must hurry and pack your bags."

"And didn't I pack them this morning. 'Tis only you and the 'orses wot's 'oldin' up the parade."

THE DRIVE TO AMBERLEIGH seemed endless. They spent a brief time at a wayside inn to refresh the horses and sleep for a few hours before continuing their journey. It was late the next day when they arrived unannounced. Much to Udora's surprise, Mrs. Kragen had the household running smoothly. She was happy to see them but obviously disappointed that the girls had remained behind. Udora contrived to satisfy her with tales of their adventures in Town.

It was with some effort that she escaped the woman's curiosity and summoned a servant to take a message to Aaron at Partridge Run. She would see him on the morrow. At Amberleigh. It came as an afterthought but good sense told her that a confrontation on her own grounds would present an advantage. And she needed every advantage she could muster.

Amberleigh seemed to enfold her within its walls. She touched the polished wood, the shimmering crystal candelabra, the lustrous patina of silver and pewter that decorated the walls and tables. From the window she saw the sweep of lawn and trees leading to the river. How inviting it looked in the late afternoon sunshine. The treetops of Deep Spring Park were barely visible beyond the bend in the river. And a bit farther, concealed from her view by the dense foliage, lay Partridge Run. . .and Aaron Bently.

The anger that she felt towards him had cooled somewhat. It lay like a solid lump in her midsection, more pain than anger now that she had had time to consider his actions. In truth, it was not unusual for marriages to be based on the need to acquire property or funds to finance the upkeep of an ancestral home. Her own first marriage settlement had bolstered her father's faltering income at a difficult time in his life. Fortunately Fate intervened and she quite fell in love with Thurgood Hendricks, God rest his soul.

Aaron Bently had no reason to marry for money. Property was another thing. To some men the lust for property was even stronger than their desire for a beautiful woman. In any case, he could hold his breath for an enternity before she would let him win this test of wills. She would get Ulysses back one way or another and she would never give up control of Deep Springs Park.

The following morning Udora heard a gig pull up on the gravelled drive. It was just like Aaron to arrive a few minutes early, devil take the man. She would make him cool his heels until she was ready to see him.

Udora had been at her wit's end trying to decide what to wear. She had finally chosen a beautifully understated gown of grey velvet with white satin cuffs and a matching collar piped in grey. Maggie glanced at the dress and flopped down in a chair.

"I always knowed you'd take leave o' your senses. 'Tis not the vicar who's come' to call."

"Whatever do you mean? It's not as if I'm dressing for some assignation. This is a meeting to transact business."

"Be that as it may, m'lady, but a wee bit o' *dis*traction can only 'elp you in the *trans*action. There's not a man alive what can concentrate when there's a bit o' bosom peekin' out to catch 'is eye."

"Perhaps you are right. What would you suggest?"

"The black lace wi' the bodice cut to 'ere," she said, drawing her hands down to a spot near her waistline.

Udora laughed. "Maggie, you are too bad by half. I don't want him dragging me off to my boudoir."

"Sure you don't. I'd bet me mother's life you'd be the first one up the stairs should 'e so much as suggest it."

"Enough, Maggie. You go too far. Besides, your mother has already passed on." She put her hand to her cheek. "I believe I'll settle for the green sprigged muslin," she said, ignoring the sly look on Maggie's face. The muslin was only a shade above decent for this time of day, but it certainly served to make her feel young and joyful. Perhaps it would lift her mood of nervous apprehension.

She kept Aaron waiting a full twenty minutes before she deigned to join him downstairs. To her surprise, the caller was not Aaron but a liveried servant bearing a message. He rose, hat in hand, and bowed when she entered.

"My lady, his lordship has sent me to inform you that he has been detained. He requests that you accept his apology and begs you to consider meeting him at Partridge Run as soon as possible."

"I'll do no such thing! What could be so pressing that he is forced to put off our meeting?"

The messenger, an intellingent-looking young lad of perhaps fifteen years, turned scarlet from the tip of his freckled ears to his skinny neck. "I believe, my lady, that one of his prize sheep is giving birth. My lord asked me to escort you to the stable."

"Oh, very well. I suppose I must do as he ordains. I have no wish to delay my return to London because some barnyard animal has decided to give birth." She motioned him to wait outside. "I'll get my cloak."

The warmth of the barn was comforting after facing the chilly breeze on the short ride to Partridge Run. It was dark inside except for sunlight filtering through the chinks in the wood and a circle of light where three men were gathered around a stool. Aaron, seated on the stool, was holding a tiny lamb in the folds of a clean, soft rug. He was apparently attempting to feed it but the lamb refused to take milk from the dipper. Its bleating cries sounded like that of a newborn human. Udora's heart contracted. Despite her determination to be strong, she wanted nothing more than to gather Aaron, lamb and all, into her arms. Her mouth tightened. His was a calculated move, she suspected. Devil take the man, he knew her weakness for helpless animals.

Bently looked up as she approached. He seemed haggard, his shoulders limp, his eyes dark and unfathomable, his mouth a thin line beneath his moustache. He inclined his head. "Forgive me for not rising, your ladyship."

She nodded to the other men, farm lackeys, she decided. "Did the mother not survive?" she asked, returning her gaze to Aaron.

"The ewe lives but she refuses to suckle her lamb. Nor will he take milk from a rag or dipper." Bently soaked a strip of cloth in the dipper of milk and tried to get the lamb to nurse. At first it appeared to work but the lamb refused to swallow. He swore a colourful oath then looked up sharply.

"Take off one of your gloves, Udora."

"I beg your pardon."

"And I'll be needing the pin from your bonnet."

Udora did as she was told. Moments later her favourite doeskin glove was full of milk and the lamb was sucking at if it was the most natural thing to do. With a sigh of satisfaction Bently turned the lamb over to the care of the stableboy and cleaned his hands in a pan of fresh water.

He turned to Udora. "Forgive my abruptness. I should have asked for your glove, not demanded it." He took her by the arm and guided her into another room.

Udora gave him a wry look as she peeled of the other glove. "You might as well have this one, too."

"Thank you. I hope they were not too costly."

"I wouldn't know, actually. They were a gift from Princess Caroline."

"I had no idea. Please accept my apology and if there is anything I can do to repay you, your wish is my command."

She looked at him sharply, shaking the glove in front of him. "For this? There is no need to apologize. But since you are in a generous mood, I would that you'd forgo this nonsense about Ulysses and Snowball and release him forthwith."

He was so close that when he turned to look down at her his arm brushed her breast and she drew in her breath.

"Is that why you returned to Coventry, Udora? To retrieve your cat?" He put his hands on her shoulders and held her none too gently.

She lifted her head to look into his eyes. It was a mistake. Her mouth was suddenly dry and she darted her tongue across her lips to moisen them. "Wh-what other reason c-could I possibly have?"

He chuckled softly. "Perhaps this, Udora. Perhaps this."

Before she could resist he bent and kissed her. This time it was no casual peck on the cheek. He covered her mouth with his.

CHAPTER TWELVE

HIS MOUSTACHE feathered across her upper lip, sending a shower of sparks through her veins. He brushed the corners of her mouth, traced the outer edges of her lips and slowly moved his head from side to side in a dance of the senses.

She half-heartedly tried to resist, but he held her with such gentle firmness that she soon lost the desire to move. Udora was appalled by her own traitorous response. When he lifted his head she met his gaze with unqualified yearning. He chuckled deep in his throat.

"Now tell me, Udora. We both recognize that something untoward has transpired between us. Wasn't this the true reason you returned to Coventry?"

"I don't know what you mean."

His eyes glittered. "Don't play the innocent with me. Of course you know what I mean." His gaze moved from her face down to the swell of her breasts where the gown was cut to reveal their pale perfection. Then once again his gaze met hers and a smile crossed his face. "You even dressed the part, my love. You knew that no man could turn away from such an invitation."

"Invitation, my eyes! I gave you no such thing."

His smile widened. She took one look at the self-satisfaction written on his face and would have struck him, but he was holding her wrist.

"Unhand me at once!"

"Not until you admit that you enjoyed the kiss as much as I did."

"Never!"

"Then perhaps we should try again. I suspect you're out of practice."

Udora gasped as he pulled her against him, but any objection she might have had was lost when his mouth covered hers.

It took time, a few more kisses and sheer desperation to give her strength. When he released his hold for a moment, Udora gathered her skirt and ran for the door, slamming it shut and throwing the wooden bar over it. She bolted for the outer door, knowing that Aaron would have to go the long way round to follow after her.

But once again he outwitted her. When she opened the stable door he was standing there arms crossed, feet spread wide, waiting.

"Now then, my lady. Shall we talk?"

Udora leaned against the doorframe and sighed. "You have a very physical way of talking...and of putting words into my mouth."

"Deny it all you wish, Udora, but you cannot hide your true feelings from me. I know you care for me."

"Smug bastard!" Udora said.

He raised an eyebrow. "It isn't like you to cast aspersions on my parentage...but...considering your present lack of control, I'm sure they would have forgiven you."

"It seems to me that you are the one who lacks control."

"On the contrary. I had every intention of kissing you. This was no sudden impulse. I've thought about it, wanted it, indeed, needed it, every hour, every minute since the last time I held you in my arms."

She felt herself weakening then pulled back sharply. "No. No, Aaron. You've always been able to talk the hind leg off a bird. I knew it the first time I saw you talk the maids into keeping the windows washed and fresh flowers in your workroom, and the way you always manoeuvre the girls into finishing their lessons." She hugged her arms around her waist in a gesture of defense.

"You are too clever for me, Aaron. I—I trusted you. I had no idea that the only reason you wanted me was to gain control over Deep Springs Park."

"Surely you can't believe that, my love."

"Ah, but I do and therein lies the rub. I could never marry you knowing you had ulterior motives in currying my favour."

"What can I do to convince you that you are wrong?"

"I don't know, Aaron. I just don't know." She dabbed at her eyes with a square of linen. "I really must be going now. Would you be so good as to hand Ulysses over to me?"

"As you wish. I think you will find him in an empty stall to your right."

Once her eyes were again used to the semidarkness, Udora retraced her steps with Bently following after her. "Look there, in the manger," he said, pointing to the far end of the stall.

Udora lifted her skirt and entered the clean-swept enclosure. Sweet-smelling hay filled the stable rack and overflowed onto the floor. Udora's heart contracted when she saw Ulysses curled into a contented ball alongside Snowball. He looked up and purred when she stroked his back, but he made no move to come to her. She put her hand under him to lift him, but he made a warning sound deep in his throat.

She was stricken. "What have you done to my cat?"

Bently looked at her and shook his head. "What have I done, Udora? Nothing. Nothing at all. Ulysses simply answered a call that was too strong to resist." He put his hand on her shoulder. "Do you still want to take him to London?"

She stood silently for a moment, then shook her head. "No. I think not. It's too late, isn't it? If you will excuse me now, I must be going."

"Udora, wait. You don't have to go."

"No. I must return to London today." She was careful not to look back.

WHEN MAGGIE HAD SEEN the look of utter despair on Udora's face she wisely refrained from questioning her but made haste to repack the valises. Only a few times before had Maggie seen her mistress so distraught and then it was on the death of a husband. A further comparison was drawn when Udora took to wearing black when she returned to The Lark's Nest. It seemed as if she had no spark for living or even to choose costumes which would lift her mood.

The girls became subdued after their initial eagerness to welcome her home. Topaz curled up on a settee, pulling her legs up beneath her, a position that would normally have set Udora's temper to simmer. But Udora appeared not to notice. The girls looked at one another in surprise. When she spoke, Udora sounded tired.

"Now, young ladies, tell me what you've been doing while I was in the country."

Emerald turned the page of her book and marked it with a silk ribbon. "Mr. Bonaventure, our new tutor, is a fairly decent chap. His French is quite good and he is teaching us to play the harp." She frowned. "But you must know that his knowledge of Elizabethan history is appalling."

Taz snorted in an unladylike fashion. "Oh, my deah . . . what a tragedy!"

"And he gave us each a copy of *Mangnall's Questions*," Amy said, "so that we can be prepared to carry on proper conversations." She twisted a honey-coloured ringlet around her finger. "But I like Monsieur le Tellier better. He knows all the latest dances and is ever so much lighter on his feet than poor Mr. Andulay."

Topaz chuckled. "And he smells better. I think he wears honey water."

Amy gave Topaz a look which silenced her. "Would you like us to show you the new dance steps we learned, my lady?"

"Not now, dear girl. I think I shall lie down for a time. Why don't you run along and ask Maggie to fix a hot bath for me?"

Emmy and Amy disappeared as quickly as if let off their lead but Topaz remained behind. Rising and taking a chair next to Udora, Topaz leaned forward.

"Did you have a battle royal with Bently, then?"

Udora was taken aback. "Whatever makes you say such a thing?"

"You look most awful. The way Mummy used to when she wanted to cry. Like when Papa first brought me from the convent to live with them."

It was the look of sadness that washed over Topaz's normally mischievous face that stirred something in Udora. She reached out her hands. "My dear child, you see far too much for such a young woman. Yes, to be honest, Lord Kesterson and I did not come to terms. We have decided to go our separate ways. Some things just aren't meant to be."

"Then Maggie was wrong."

"Maggie? What did she say to you?"

"She said that you taught her that if two people were meant to be together, nothing could keep them apart. Was it a falsehood, then?"

Udora leaned back against the cushions and sighed. "Not a falsehood, certainly, but one can't allow for misjudgements."

"Meaning that you misjudged Bently's character?"

"So it would seem."

"I don't think so, my lady. Perhaps it is more a question of misunderstanding. He's always been kind and honest with the three of us. Maybe you are at fault for not listening to him. You are very quick tempered and stubborn, you know, and judgemental."

Udora straightened, her eyes blazing. It took a moment for her to compose herself. "That will be quite enough, Miss Topaz. I suggest you go to your room and study Mrs. Chapon's book, *Improvement of the*

Mind. Specifically the passages dealing with respect towards your elders."

Topaz curtsied and started towards the door. Typically she turned to fire a last-minute salvo. "You can punish me if you wish, but I told the truth. Sometimes you don't listen."

Udora got up and paced the room. At least the wretched girl had accomplished one thing. She had made her angry. That in itself had served to dilute the soup of depression in which she had allowed herself to stew.

Well, no more. She didn't need Aaron. She didn't need any man. It wasn't as if she were to be consigned to the rank of Ape Leader. Certainly not after having been married four times. And she wouldn't be lonely, not with all the work involved in the girls' Court Presentation. Indeed, there was hardly a moment to spare.

Maggie was filling the cosmetic pots in Udora's dressing table when she came into the rooms. She took one look at Udora and dropped a powderpuff. "Lord o' mercy! Herself has come back to life."

"And that's quite enough of that, my girl," Udora said, flinging her shawl on the bed. "We have work to do. I want my entire wardrobe gone over. Look for my slippers," she said flinging open the armoire door. "You've let them become scuffed and shabby. How can we get back into Society when you've done little but sip tea and dally with the hired hands."

Maggie raised her gaze to the ceiling and mumbled. "Methinks I liked 'er better when she was gone to seed."

Udora would have chastised her, but she saw the smile that lit her abigail's eyes. Maggie, who often accompanied her to parties and routs, loved it when they entertained. Moreover, Udora realized suddenly, Maggie wanted her to be happy. For all their differences there was a bond between them that grew stronger with each passing year.

INVITATIONS HAD BEGUN to collect in a surprisingly large heap while Udora was at Amberleigh and in the short time since her return. Many of them were for balls and routs which Udora considered a bit too extreme for her, considering she was currently without benefit of escort. But a dozen or more were for afternoon teas and garden parties to which the girls, along with Maggie and Sally, accompanied her. Shy at first, the girls soon learned to adapt to Polite Society. Of course, Taz was always the queer card. That she was capable of anything, Udora was quite aware. When Udora complimented her behaviour after one particularly gruelling party, Taz looked at her with a calculated gaze.

"I'm trying to keep my side of the bargain."

"The bargain?"

"You haven't forgotten your promise to let me ride in a balloon?" she demanded.

"No, my dear, but I hoped you had." Udora smiled, patting her hair.

Taz fixed her with a leaden gaze and refused comment.

The one invitation over which Udora agonized was from Yvette Waverly. She and Lord Bancroft were giving a grand ball to open the Season. If it were just anyone Udora wouldn't have hesitated to decline but because of Yvette's lying-in and the subsequent birth of their child, this was the first time in over a year that they had found it possible to entertain in the lavish manner which they both so enjoyed. Besides, Yvette had insisted that Udora be present. Out of affection for the girls, Yvette had planned a separate dance party for the young set so that the Thackery girls could apply what they had learned from their dancemaster.

Udora would attend of course—she could hardly do otherwise—but when it came to selecting a gown, nothing could have interested her less. She offhandedly suggested the ivory satin when Maggie pressed her for a decision, but upon hearing Maggie's disdainful sniff, Udora knew at once that it wouldn't do.

"What is it now, Maggie?"

"Oh, nothin'." She saw the look on Udora's face and hastened to add. "But iffen 'twas me what put on a few extra pounds I wouldn'a wear a gown wot makes it plain as a pikestaff. But o' course you can't see what's behind you, so's it don't matter none. 'Specially, seein' as 'ow you ain't put yourself back on the Marriage Mart."

"Of course it matters. Not for myself, you understand, but I must maintain my dignified position for the girls' sake."

Maggie slanted a look across at Udora and opened a copy of *Bell's Court*. "I just happened onto a pattern wot might look fair on you, considerin' ev'rythin'."

Udora glanced at the drawing and was immediately enthralled. "It's beautiful. What do you mean fair? It would look splendid on me."

"Well, I'm sure I wouldn'a go so far as to say that but we could make do wi' it."

"Don't be a goose. It's perfect and you know it. I think I'll use the bolt of Capucine silk and add insets of Nakara satin in the sleeves." She tapped her cheek. "And what do you think of pearl and diamond beading here on the bodice where the sleeves go off the shoulders?"

"'Tis just what I thought," Maggie said smugly.

Udora stared at her. If she had suspected it before, now she knew what Maggie was about. It seemed that everyone was taking great pains to get her mind off Aaron Bently. Their concern touched her, but it didn't serve. He was always there inside her, a silent ache that never seemed to go away.

THE WEATHER BODED ILL for the Bancroft grand ball. It had rained nearly every day for three weeks since the invitations had gone out. Miraculously at two o'clock that afternoon, the weather cleared and a brilliant sun burned off the surface dampness. The girls looked terribly grown up in their new gowns, and they seemed to be on their best behaviour. The fits of giggles and messages passed behind gloved hands Udora laid to the fact that this was their first big affair. Maggie and Sally were under orders to keep close watch over them, and Topaz in particular, whose gaze never rested long in one place. The girl was a challenge and yet, admittedly, a source of great joy, Udora thought. Fortunately the twins were less adventurous.

McMasters had contrived by means of several coats of fresh varnish to bring the carriage back to its original splendour, and when they arrived at the Bancroft estate Udora was only mildly uncomfortable. Yvette had invited them to arrive early, knowing that Udora would feel awkward attending without benefit of escort.

They were greeted by a row of liveried footmen wearing the Bancroft colours of burgundy and gold. Even Topaz failed to hide her amazement when she saw the glittering chandeliers, the masses of flowers that filled the marble urns and the floors which had been rubbed to a high sheen. The house smelled of beeswax polish and fresh-picked roses blending with the subtle hint of perfumed air.

Yvette, her golden hair bound with a silk rope into a crown of curls, floated down the twin staircase as if she were made of gossamer lace. The matching necklace and eardrops of pink pearls and diamonds that Andrew, Lord Bancroft, had given her on the first anniversary of their marriage looked stunning against her gown of iridescent amaranthus. Seeing that they had arrived, she pressed her hands together in pleasure.

"My dears, how charming you look. I'm sure the gossips will be hard-pressed to decide whom among you they should admire first."

Udora's smile reflected the pride she felt in the way the girls were beginning to blossom. "I'm sure much of the credit goes to you Yvette and to the countess for taking them under your wing."

They were directed to the small drawing room where a few young people were already practicing their dance steps under the watchful eye of an instructor. A group of young men, still fresh from their first year at Oxford or Cambridge turned as if on cue to survey the girls. Udora noted with satisfaction that they did not turn away. One tall youth in particular set his sights on Topaz. He made a comment to the boy standing next to him and was promptly given a shove in her direction. He stopped, then apparently summoned courage and started toward her again. Taz saw what had transpired and raised her eyes to the ceiling.

Udora remonstrated with her. "Now, Topaz, try to be considerate. Thoughtfulness is the first mark of a lady, don't you know."

"And 'tis good practice," Maggie added.

Udora spread her fan in front of her mouth and leaned towards Maggie. "I've asked Sally to look after Miss Emerald and Miss Amy. I'll leave Miss Topaz to you."

Maggie curtsied and smiled wickedly. "Yes, m'lady. I'll try to keep 'er from liftin' 'er petticoats."

Udora sighed and shook her head. Heaven protect them, but most of her sympathy went to the young man. He was as well as done for.

Upon leaving the petite ballroom, Udora was instantly struck by how separate she felt. People had begun to arrive by the dozens. Couples all, save for old Mrs. Wendallhurst carrying her two yapping dogs. Gossip had it that she left everything to them in her will. They already wore more diamonds on their collars than most women could claim for their first marriage. Udora nodded to her and moved away before the dogs could sniff her arm.

It was a move she regretted. Lady Sylvia Montweeden nearly collided with her as she passed through the doorway. Each forced a laugh. "Ah, then, Lady Udora. How nice to see you!" she exclaimed in her high, little girl's voice. "You've met my Bunny, haven't you?"

Udora inclined her head towards Lord Buntingford but had no chance to greet him before Lady Sylvia continued. "My dear, you surely can't be alone? But then I suppose you must be, considering the recent and unfortunate dissolution of your betrothal. Pity. Charles was such a catch. I'm told he's seeing that horrid little Pendleton heiress."

"Now nice. I hear she's quite lovely."

"And not a day over seventeen. Perhaps that's why..." she said, pretending to ponder the reason for the broken engagement. "But of course not. You have far more to offer a man... in a, um... mature sort of way. Isn't that right, Bunny?"

"Rath...er!" he drawled, ogling Udora's not insignificant cleveage.

Sylvia turned a bright shade of pink which was more than just a reflection of her overpowering red gown. "If you will excuse us, Udora, my dear, we must move on. I promised the duchess a few moments ago that I would speak with her in the conservatory before the dancing begins." She touched her fan to her cheek. "Perhaps my Bunny would sign your card so that you won't have to sit out alone this evening."

Udora forced a smile. "How kind, but isn't it a pity! There's not one tiny dance left on my entire card. Another time, Bunny dear." She pasted a conspiratorial look on her face. "And Bunny dear, I do thank you for the other night. We must do it again soon."

He turned red from the top of his neatly folded cravat *en cascade* to the tips of his ears. Sylvia's jaw dropped a good two inches before she whisked him away.

Yvette touched Udora's arm. "My dear, what was that all about? What did you say to put our dear Bunny into such a bother?"

Udora's dimples flashed. "I merely thanked him for a pleasant evening."

"But...but...Udora, I know you wouldn't be caught with him in a room of fewer than twenty people."

"Precisely! But our dear Sylvia doesn't know that."

The women looked at each other and laughed. When she regained her composure, Yvette guided Udora towards the ballroom. "The dancing is about to begin, my dear. I want you there when Andrew leads me onto the floor."

"I couldn't. It's just too embarrassing to sit with the dowagers and I spent so long with the girls that I haven't had a moment to circulate and find someone to sign my card."

"*Nom de Dieu!* That is not a consideration. The men will swarm around you like bees to honey. Three times Charles Willingsly made me promise that you would be here tonight."

"And what about his young Miss Pendleton?"

"Penelope?" Yvette blew at the tips of her fingers. "Like that she will disappear if he thinks he has another chance at you." She lifted one elegant eyebrow. "Tell me, does he?"

"Not a single one."

Yvette looked pleased. "I thought not. Then never fear, my dearest. All is well. Aha...here is my sweet husband come to dance with me. I trust you will join us in a moment?" she said, looking over Udora's shoulder.

Something about the way Andrew winked at Udora as the couple floated onto the floor made Udora turn to look behind her. Her breath caught in her throat. Common sense told her it couldn't be, but it was.

Aaron Bently. Here in London. Coming towards her with that "may I have the pleasure of this dance" look in his eyes. But no. Whatever he had in mind went deeper than that, for the intensity of his gaze was so compelling that conversations halted and people turned to watch him confront her. Only Yvette and Andrew continued to dance. Udora was vaguely aware of their conspiratorial smiles.

So long had she forgotten to breathe that Udora was close to fainting. Bently saw that the colour had left her face, and he took her arm. "Are you all right, Udora? I didn't mean to frighten you."

She drew a deep breath and made an effort to calm herself. "Don't be absurd. Why should I be frightened? What are you doing here, Aaron? Have you come to take possession of my other cats?"

A smile lighted his eyes. "I thought perhaps we could share them. And the girls."

"What are you saying?" she blustered.

"Perhaps we could dance. We seem to be under rather serious scrutiny." Before she could comment, he put his arm around her and waltzed her onto the floor. As if by a secret signal others joined them on the dance floor.

Udora looked up at him, very much aware of his immaculate black velvet dress coat, and the diamond stud in his frilled cravat. How could she have ever imagined that he was nothing more than a country bailiff?

He held her close and then closer. Udora schooled herself to ignore the message his body was sending out to her but to no avail. She felt her face turn pink. "I asked you a question, Aaron. What are you doing here?"

He held her away from him for the briefest of seconds, then once again pulled her close. "Ah, Udora. Haven't you guessed?" He pressed his lips to her forehead, ignoring the gasp which went up from the matrons seated on the sidelines. "It's as uncomplicated as this, my love. Just like Ulysses, I simply answered a call I couldn't resist. I came for you."

Udora laughed shakily and blinked back the tears. "Mind you, I'm not admitting that Ulysses was guilty of any wrongdoing, but is it your intention to also hold me as hostage?"

"Only if it becomes necessary. It is my sincere hope that you will choose to hold *my* freedom in *your* hands . . . for the rest of our lives."

"I—I—" She shook her head in bewilderment.

"Hush. Let's enjoy the dance."

It occurred to her for the first time that Aaron Bently was dancing. Dancing! He who had flatly refused to set foot on the dance floor. She tensed and missed a step. He looked down at her.

"Out of practice, my lady?"

She smiled. "What's happened? Your limp is scarcely noticeable. You dance very well." Only then did she notice the sweat beading his forehead and begin to suspect how much the effort was costing him.

"Come, Aaron. Let's find someplace where we can talk."

He led her off the floor to a secluded alcove, much to the disappointment of the onlookers. "We could have continued for a while longer, Udora. The muscles in my leg are becoming stronger each day since I've been frequenting the baths at Leamington."

She tightened her hand on his arm. "You did this for me, Aaron? I—I am overwhelmed. No one, nothing... has ever touched me so deeply."

He looked relieved and yet apprehensive as he seated her next to him on a settee in the shadows of an enormous potted palm. "I missed you, Udora. I want to marry you." She started to say something but he held up his hands. "No, wait. I know what you're thinking. You are still overset about Deep Springs Park."

He saw her eyes darken and he hurriedly withdrew a paper from inside his coat. "Although I cannot deny that I want the park to be once more adjoined to the oak grove at Partridge Run, it occurred to me that by giving you the deed to that section of oak trees, the grant would be restored to its original size. It is a small spit of land compared to the rest of Partridge Run and Amberleigh, but it is a jewel of a piece of property and should not remain divided." He placed the document in her hands. "And whether or not you choose to accept my offer of marriage, the deed will always remain in your name and, if you wish, may revert to the estate of Amberleigh in due course."

Udora was almost too surprised to speak. "I cannot accept this, Aaron. The title to Deep Springs Park will only become mine when the girls marry or reach their majority, or so I understand. And besides, the oak grove is a part of your family heritage."

"Nothing is important to me if it keeps the two of us apart." He took her hands in his and held them to his lips. "You accepted my proposal of marriage once before. I know you care for me, Udora. Tell me I'm not mistaken."

A smile flitted across her face. "You're not mistaken. I do have a certain degree of affection for you, but at the same time I find you quite insufferable."

He pulled back and studied her face, his moustache twitching, for it was clear to him that she returned his love in full measure. "There are some concessions I am prepared to make, my love. We could, for example, share ownership of Snowball's kittens once they are born. And of course, I would insist that you allow me to share the guardianship of the three girls."

She tilted her head. "I suppose we could agree on that, but there is a question of where to live. It is imperative that I take up residence in Town during the Season, at least until the girls are launched into Society."

"Did I mention that I am quite willing to remove to London during their come-out and that I own a rather nice house in Great Stanhope Street? You would, I think find it a suitable place for the girls to entertain prospective suitors."

Udora swallowed her surprise at the exclusive address. She made an effort to sound casual. "I think it might do." She put her hand on his arm. "Have I told you, Mr. Bently, that you are a very brave man?"

"For asking to contribute to the guardianship of the three girls? I think not. At least not since you have taken them under your wing. They have grown into decent young ladies."

"I refer to the fact that you would become number five."

He stroked his moustache. "Ah, yes. That fact did escape me. Perhaps I should make one stipulation, Udora."

"Indeed?"

"And that is that you allow me to live at least until you tire of me."

"And just how long are you prepared to keep me amused?"

"Forever, if need be."

Her eyes misted. "Forever is a lovely word." She pressed his hand to her lips. "Consider it done, my lord. Consider it done."

The quintessential small town, where everyone knows everybody else!

Finally, books that capture the pleasure of tuning in to your favorite TV show!

GREAT READING...GREAT SAVINGS...AND A FABULOUS FREE GIFT!

Each book set in Tyler is a self-contained love story; together, the twelve novels stitch the fabric of the community. The covers honor the old American tradition of quilting; each cover depicts a patch of the large Tyler quilt.

With Tyler you can receive a fabulous gift, ABSOLUTELY FREE, by collecting proofs-of-purchase found in each Tyler book. And use our special Tyler coupons to save on your next TYLER book purchase.

Join your friends at Tyler for the seventh book, ARROWPOINT by Suzanne Ellison, available in September.

Rumors fly about the death at the old lodge! What happens when Renata Meyer finds an ancient Indian sitting cross-legged on her lawn?

If you missed *Whirlwind* (March), *Bright Hopes* (April), *Wisconsin Wedding* (May), *Monkey Wrench* (June), *Blazing Star* (July) or *Sunshine* (August) and would like to order them, send your name, address, zip or postal code, along with a check or money order for $3.99 for each book ordered (please do not send cash), plus 75¢ postage and handling ($1.00 in Canada), payable to Harlequin Reader Service, to:

In the U.S.
3010 Walden Avenue
P.O. Box 1325
Buffalo, NY 14269-1325

In Canada
P.O. Box 609
Fort Erie, Ontario
L2A 5X3

Please specify book title(s) with your order.
Canadian residents add applicable federal and provincial taxes.

TYLER-7

COMING NEXT MONTH

#81 THE UGLY DUCKLING by Brenda Hiatt
Miss Deirdre Wheaton was in a pucker. She had fallen heel over ears in love with Lord Wrotham but learned, much to her dismay, that in order to follow her heart, she would have to abandon her soul.

#82 THE ABSENTEE EARL by Clarice Peters
One year had passed since Viola Challerton, Lady Avery, had been deserted by her husband of a mere two hours, the Earl of Avery. She had not expected Richard ever to return, but when he did, she found that little had changed, except for herself!